M000164143

Rational Women

Stories

Randy Kraft

©All rights reserved.
Published in the United States by Maple57 Press
2020
www.Maple57Press.com
ISBN: 978-0-9973791-3-6
Library of Congress Registration: TXu 2-172-993

Randy Kraft
randykraftwriter.com

*No part of this book may be reproduced or used in any form
without permission from the author.*

Cover Art by Bea Aaronson
San Miguel de Allende, MX
www.artlifebea.com

Cover Design by David Smith
www.designdsmith.com

Also by Randy Kraft
COLORS OF THE WHEEL
SIGNS OF LIFE

These stories were previously published:
An Anonymous Woman in *Typishly*
The Disbelieving Daughter titled *Rest in Peace*
in *Jewish Literary Journal*
The Jaded Journalist titled *Pas de Deux*
in *Parhelion Magazine*
The Sculptor titled *Only Now*
in Literary Mama.

*All stories are works of fiction. Any similarities to real people or
situations are unintentional, or intended with great affection.*

Rational Women

The being cannot be termed rational or virtuous, who obeys any authority but that of reason.

Mary Wollstonecraft

If we admit that human life can be ruled by reason, then all possibility of life is destroyed.

Leo Tolstoy

An Anonymous Woman

She glanced out the hotel window. Not much to see. She has glanced out this window every day this week – nothing of note and nothing different beyond the shade of the sky. Her room faced an unremarkable side street off a boulevard radiating from the Bahnhof, the train station. The one visual interest – the dome crowning that plaza – faced the grand lake flanking the Alstadt, the historic center of Lucerne, Switzerland, where she planned to wander this late afternoon.

A hint of pink light shimmered beyond the dome, the sky nearly cobalt blue along the rim. Autumn days make for cozy evenings, but rush the traveler. She had already scoffed a late lunch, filed her post-conference report and dispatched the last emails. Workweek concluded. She snapped the laptop closed. Rather than relief, she had the familiar sensation of disconnection that shadows her through restless weekends. And she was tired. She never sleeps well anymore. Nevertheless, she was determined to stretch her legs and see the sights, even if she'd rather burrow under the duvet on the soft feather bed watching English language television.

As she turned from the window, she noticed a man gazing from a window opposite. He peered down to the street from the upper floor of a modest building marked by a flat façade, tall narrow windows and a steep roofline. Architecture meant to suggest a seriousness of purpose. Although his features were vague, he stood tall, he wore a pale shirt, white or blue, no tie or jacket, and he had graying, perhaps blonde hair. Likely a businessman – a fellow work machine rejoicing, or bracing himself, for another Friday night.

She had come to Lucerne to attend an industry conference, the first since she relocated to England. The closing meeting ended Friday midday so participants might make trains and planes to return to their homes before nightfall. All week they had been confined to artificially lit seminar rooms, buried as if in a crypt while the Alps loomed on the perimeter like mythological gods. She had caught a glimpse of the lake only on the day she arrived. Midweek, when most of the eighty participants broke for a historic walking tour, she declined, ostensibly to review her notes. Now she has the time, and the inclination, to explore, and a weekend here far preferable to another weekend alone in her flat.

She stored her attaché case and laptop under the bed and switched from the charcoal gray silk blouse she wore over black slacks into a plum merino V-neck sweater, another of the dark colors she wears that are nearly black, but not black, then took a brush through her shoulder-length brown hair and dabbed a bit of bronzer on her cheeks, if only to appear a little less worn out to herself.

With a complementary shade of scarf around her neck, she grabbed jacket and purse and glanced once more to the window across the street. The man was no longer in sight, like an apparition, and she had to shake off a surprising sense of disappointment.

She might have taken one steep flight of stairs to the lobby, but she stepped instead into the square lift, pulling the accordion metal gate to seal her inside. As a rule, she avoids cramped spaces, and these old elevators feel like prison cells; however today the snug space seemed an embrace and she has learned to take comfort wherever she finds it.

At the reception desk, she dropped off the room key – an oversized iron relic that might have fit the lock of a 16th century dungeon. Perhaps an artifact of the reformation, she imagined, hung from a brass ring to discourage guests from taking the key with them. The desk clerk took stock of her, without recognition. She was one of the few not staying at the larger hotel hosting the conference and all week she had dashed out early mornings and slipped back in the evenings, without engaging with staff the way other visitors do.

All well, Madam? the clerk asked, with a well-trained smile.

Yes, she answered with a pronounced nod and the clerk echoed the nod and wished her a pleasant evening. *To you as well,* she responded, as she stepped out of the hotel and headed toward the corner in the direction of the lake. When she stopped at the crosswalk, she saw the man, as discernible as if she knew him, waiting with a cluster of pedestrians for the signal to cross. He wore a black three-quarter-length coat, unbuttoned in the cool, not yet cold air. A style of coat that hugs the shoulders and makes a man seem sturdy. She saw now the shirt was blue and his hair like polished silver. A black leather messenger bag, streaked with age, hung low from a thick strap over his chest, as if containing state secrets or, more likely, the weekend work of the overworked.

She watched him cross the street. He had long legs and a long stride, although his gait was more of an amble, as if retracing steps he has taken many times.

Without thought, or reason, she followed him.

He made his way down one long street, in the shadow of imposing buildings, before he turned and crossed over to a sidewalk parallel to the river leading to the lake. He passed, without notice, the iconic Chapel Bridge, where a throng of tourists congregated taking photographs. According to the travel notes included with the conference packet, that footbridge is the oldest of its type in Europe. Pink and purple flowers overflowed the window boxes along the length of it. She should have stopped to look closer; that was, after all, her intention for the walk. Nevertheless, she followed his lead.

Along the river, slow-moving currents tumbled like tiny rapids over a series of locks before spilling at last into the lake. This water has made its way all through this country, she thought. Other countries too. Across hillsides and rocky channels to settle at this lake. Meandering, but with intent, as she meant to be, if she were not following the man.

When he turned toward the next footbridge, where a scrolled-iron railing shed circular shadows underfoot, she was momentarily mesmerized by the pattern and might have lost sight of him, but when she looked up, there he was, a beacon of sorts, like the landmark medieval water tower she glimpsed beyond the Chapel Bridge: the eponymous lucerna.

Fortunately, he walked unhurriedly, so she was able to keep up. A chronic ache in her hip and a slight limp stalk her every move, the scar tissue penance and punishment for an accident over a year ago that left her a solo traveler.

She stopped briefly and closed her eyes to shutter the memory. A couple of consciously deep breaths usually calm her down. When she opened her eyes again, she searched out the man in the crowd and easily caught up with his unhurried stride to the cobblestone streets.

A parade of shop windows floated in her peripheral vision like the mountains beyond the lake. Tantalizing mounds of artistic notepapers, leather-bound journals, metallic pens, gleaming bejeweled watches, and the mélange of colorful home accessories piled artistically to attract shoppers. Clusters of café tables were already set out on the narrow streets, enticing weekend revelers. The old city bustled with visitors and locals en route to evening activities. Some strolled. Others rushed. They chatted with friends or into cell phones. Tourists stopped to photograph architectural elements as they gushed over chocolates melting in their mouths. The atmosphere felt like the opening scene of an opera – the throng arriving on stage from the wings all at once, ad alta voce.

The man shifted into an alley and she picked up her pace to follow. He turned again into another and at the end of this passage made an abrupt sharp turn, where he climbed a short flight of stone steps to a

French restaurant. At the foot of the steps, a wooden sign framed a blackboard announcing in blue chalk an impressive selection of Bordeaux wines and listing the specials of the day: Coq au Bin, Blanquette de Veau and Mussels Meuniere.

She imagined he must be there to meet someone – a wife, lover, friend or colleague. She stood at the bottom of the steps pretending to study the menu posted there. Why linger? What was she doing following a stranger into a strange city? She meant only to make good use of time to still her mind, see the sites and return soon enough to the next workweek. Still, her feet seemed bolted to the stone, weighted down by something more than gravity, and when she finally galvanized her legs, she turned, then stopped in her tracks, snared by an invisible force field, turned back and sprinted the steps as if she were late. As if someone expected her.

In the vestibule, she took a moment to adjust to the low lighting. She sniffed the preparatory aromas of garlic and lemon, also cigarette smoke, still common in this part of the world, as if to protest modernity. Once in focus, she saw five café tables lined up to her left, parallel to a long dark wood bar to the right. More formal dining tables were hidden on the other side of the bar. Walls were painted a soft gold, the tabletops white and gold tile with bright white napkins folded in the center into a cross, like the Swiss flag.

The man sat at a far table, the only patron; too early for a European dinner. His coat hung on a nearby rack and he chatted with a bartender serving as waiter, dressed in a crisp white shirt with a cognac-colored vest and with a white towel folded over his belt. He poured red wine from a carafe into a large stemmed glass.

One glass. One place setting. He was alone.

She observed him more closely. Handsomer than at first sight, in a Germanic way: a wide forehead, deep set dark eyes, a squared chin and ruddy cheeks. The face of nefarious Nazis in war films, also the faces of members of the resistance or sympathetic neighbors. One has to peer into their eyes to know if they are to be feared or trusted, although, even then, uncertain. Nothing seems certain now.

The man sat tall, perfectly perpendicular, his spine pressed against the leather padding. Lined up with precision like the napkins. Like the merchandise in shop windows. He seemed older than first perceived, perhaps in his early fifties, like her husband, who was ten years older than she, and although she wasn't close enough to detect, she imagined similar smile lines spreading from his eyes and tiny grooves from his lips.

She watched him. She enjoyed watching him without his knowing he was being watched. There was no host at the door, no one ushering her to a table. The bartender, busy with preparations, retrieved a bowl of nuts from behind the bar for the man, who nodded thanks as he took his first sip of the wine. He had waited for the wine to breathe. A petit verdot, she suspected or, more likely, blended with a cabernet franc, the more complex of the Bordeaux reds. He nibbled a handful of nuts and then, as he pulled from his bag a device, like an iPad, he looked up and caught sight of her. She smiled, and he smiled, a spontaneous, subtle smile, before he lowered his eyes to turn his attention to his reading.

Perhaps she was not deserving of a second glance. She's not a looker – not one to turn heads or attract attention. She had, however, captured the attention of the only man that mattered fifteen years ago and she believes lightning does not strike twice. On the other hand, the man might suppose she was there to meet someone. He might presume, as she had, that anyone alone this early in the evening must be expected.

She breathed deeply, purposefully, uncertain what she had in mind. Whatever had come over her, she gave herself to it like a narcoleptic sleepwalking through a bizarre waking dream. *Okay then*, she whispered, lifted her head high, and sauntered to his table. Without a word, she sat opposite him and hooked her purse over the back of the chair, as if she were only late for a date. He looked up with a bemused expression.

Do you speak English? she asked.

Yes, he answered.

May I join you? she asked.

It seems you have, he said.

She slipped off her jacket and hung that too across the back of the chair. She loosened the lavender scarf she wore to complement the plum not-black sweater, thinking, as she often has, if nearly black suggests the accident only nearly happened, then sitting with a stranger in a Swiss bar might be nearly rational.

Her heart beat so urgently she feared he might sense the vibration. A flush rose from her chest to her cheeks, a typical response to an awkward situation, and as she sat, attempting to still her nerves, she marveled at her audacity.

She recalled, years ago, she had noticed a young model in a newspaper ad who reminded her of herself in college. In the photo, a group of supposed students sprawled on a lawn wearing casual sporty clothes. At the time, she couldn't stop staring at the girl in the image, peeling the layers of her own life, and when she showed her husband the ad, he said the girl looked so much like her, he might seek her out to frolic with the younger version he never knew. They laughed about it. He called the young model a doppelganger, although this is also considered the harbinger of bad luck, or death. She hadn't thought about that in years, but in this surreal moment, was she another doppelganger of herself?

Where are you from? the man inquired, interrupting her random thoughts. He spoke with a clipped Germanic accent.

The states, she answered. *California, although I live in London now. I was here for a conference.*

California. What part?

North. What's called the wine country.

Ah, beautiful place. But you must miss the sun.

She wouldn't mention she had accepted the job in London specifically for the gloom, like water seeking its own level. Instead she said, in her best imitation of an American optimist, *London is the greenest city in Europe. Great parks, an abundance of trees. So I gave up the sun, not the green.*

A good compromise, he said.

She smiled. *I hate to dine alone,* she said.

The bartender, intuiting the right moment, arrived at her side. She asked him to recommend his favorite of the white Bordeaux. *Perhaps a sémillon, crisp, with a clean finish?* she inquired. He nodded appreciably and answered he would be honored to select the perfect wine.

You've made him happy, the man remarked. *He is so rarely asked to choose. People have their favorites these days.*

I prefer to rely on expertise, she answered.

Which you too seem to have.

My business is marketing California wines to the international vendors. However, she said, leaning forward to share the secret, *I prefer the French grape.*

He smiled, the warmth of that smile an invitation to relax. Her heartbeat settled into a steady pace as the bartender returned with a tulip-shaped glass on a tall stem and a bottle of white Bordeaux. He presented the label, she nodded, and he poured a tasting. She swirled, sniffed and sipped.

Perfectly chilled and perfectly balanced, she said, with a grateful smile. He poured a glass, replaced the cork, and then twisted the bottle deep into an ice bucket nearby.

I'll pay for my own, of course, she said, as the man raised his glass.

I appreciate the company, he answered.

They hesitantly leaned the tip of their glasses to clink. They sipped. They shared the sort of pleasantries strangers do: the unusually warm fall weather, the threat of global warming, the rise of wine regions throughout the world.

She noticed he wore a thick gold wedding ring, yet no wife on a Friday night. The wife too might be on a business trip, or he was, she thought, although, based on his familiarity with the bartender, he might be a regular. His wife may be gone for good, and still, the golden tether. She the same, her wedding band still on her finger. She could have explained her husband's absence, but she never speaks of it.

Confession is good for the soul, they say. Not for her. Those who needed to know – the police, family and friends – they know. They know she was the designated driver that night, because her husband suspected, correctly, there would be free-flowing wine at a birthday celebration for a friend. Ten couples, seated at a long narrow table set up on the ridge of a hill at a winery overlooking Napa Valley, enjoyed a six-course dinner with wine pairings. A balmy evening. Gentle breezes blew over them. Candles flickered down the center of the table and reflected in the wine glasses. She drank only half a glass of a pinot noir rosé, in favor of sobriety. Her husband enjoyed all the wines and was a bit giddy. He is, was, she now has to say, a silly drunk, and afterward, on the drive home, they were laughing at a laughable moment when a pick-up truck sped into an intersection plowing into the passenger side of the car far enough to hit her. She suffered a fractured hip, a broken arm and several broken ribs. Her husband bled to death before the paramedics arrived. According to the police report, the driver was intoxicated well beyond the legal limit. She was not to blame, they said.

She sat opposite the man swirling the wine, watching it slosh around the glass to breathe. A lovely color, to her eye, this wine – pale gold, like wheat or straw. She no longer drinks red, the color of blood.

The man sat quietly, watching her, waiting her out. Not one of those men compelled to impose. No need to dominate the conversation. Strangers sharing little of each other. They had not even introduced themselves, nor seemed to feel the need to.

The blush in her cheeks receded and she smiled to indicate she was ready to engage again in conversation.

Have you been here before? he asked. *This restaurant?*

No, first time. A favorite of yours?

I'm not much of a cook. Weeknights, I buy dinner at the take-away. Soups and salads, a stew. Friday night, I dine on the way home at this café. I like their mussels with frites. Fries, he translated, as if she might not know.

Sort of fish and chips, she remarked, and he laughed.

So, he lived alone, he dined alone, yet he wore a wedding ring. Kindred spirits after all, she thought.

The bartender took their dinner orders and they continued to chat, gripping the stems of their wine glasses as if ballast and sipping intermittently.

What's it like in London these days? he asked.

How do you mean?

The mood, in the shadow of Brexit.

Exasperation might be the word. The people I know have moved beyond the state of shock.

He shook his head forlornly. *I fear the transition will be much harder than suspected over time. Vast repercussions.*

The Brits are steeped in tradition. They are the quintessence of stoicism. They soldier on.

In this way, she knew, London was exactly the right place to be. The land of stoics. Her husband, of British heritage, used to say regret is a wasted emotion. So true, when there is none.

What do the Swiss think of all this? she asked.

The Swiss maintain neutrality at all times. We do our own thing, as you Americans say, as we watch our European neighbors battle their demons.

With glee?

Occasionally, although not this time. Their economic tsunami will flood the continent.

He refreshed his wine from the carafe on the table. *Have you seen much of Switzerland?*

Bern. Zurich. A side trip to Lake Constance.

Bern is my home, most of my life. My sons are there.

Beautiful city. But you live here now?

Yes. I needed a change of scene, a change of most everything. I also changed careers. My own Brexit, I suppose.

He explained that he had a long career as an international lawyer, but working now with an NGO promoting migration as a means to global economic equity. He said he travels extensively. He prefers to keep moving. He likes train travel. She bemoaned the limited train lines in the U.S. They chuckled together at the obsessive-compulsive nature of the Swiss railway.

They shared favorite cities: Paris, of course, also Budapest, Barcelona and Berlin.

The B-cities are the A-cities, he quipped.

The bartender delivered their meals and they dived in as if neither had eaten in days. They dropped empty mussel shells into a large ceramic bowl. They swept chunks of bread into the garlicky broth. They plucked crispy potatoes from tall paper cones and licked the salt off their fingers. The bartender refilled her wine glass and she thanked him again.

She became aware of the resonance of other patrons as the restaurant filled. Conversation flowed like the wine. Smoke drifted through the air on the notes of French music: a hand organ and a violin, a sultry voice. By chance, the tip of her shoe grazed his knee as she uncrossed and re-crossed her long legs, and she felt a startling jolt of desire. He said nothing and only the slightest pause suggested he noticed. The Swiss, she mused – so reserved. Thankfully, polite.

He recommended a few lesser-known museums she might enjoy and urged a boat ride on the lake. *For the tourists, yes, but enchanting, particularly this time of year.*

They shared a crème brulée, perfectly browned and crisp on top. He ordered espresso, which the waiter delivered in a copper pot turned upside-down to drip the old-fashioned way. They chatted a while longer, then she poured the coffee into the two small porcelain cups served with slivers of lemon to flavor the rims. Afterward, the bartender presented brandy in two large snifters, with his compliments.

The man said, *he is pleased to see me with a companion. The Swiss have a reputation for reserve, but we are romantics at heart.*

He blushed. She smiled. The wine and brandy settled over her body like a soft blanket. She rarely drinks anymore, beyond tasting. She has forgotten this feeling, this penetrating pleasure: the pleasure of fine food and wine, the pleasure of good company. The proximity of an attractive man.

When they left the restaurant, cobblestones shimmered under street lamps and beneath the canopy of a midnight-blue sky. Frivolity permeated the old town. When she shivered in the chill, he held her jacket for her to slip on. Although he kept a proper distance, his fingers grazed her shoulders and she felt again the titillation of touch.

Would you like an escort to the hotel? he asked.

Her heart began to race again. She imagined them in her hotel room: the slow unfastening of clothes, the first touch of skin. The tender introduction to unfamiliar bodies or, more likely, the rushed coupling of two people starved for affection. She has always enjoyed the clandestine nature of sex in hotels. Her honeymoon was an erotic revelation and, now and then, her husband booked a hotel room near his office for the grand seduction. The pretense of anonymity an aphrodisiac.

Her body craved a stronger body. Her fingers yearned for tougher skin. She felt a stirring deep down in the part of her also buried. She thought she might weep for the longing.

On the other hand, Lucerne is a city where a woman is safe to walk alone, he added, to suggest the virtue in his offer.

He took her hand and brought it to his lips to kiss her palm. She saw her wedding band glisten in the lamplight like a neon sign: no, not yet. She smiled and withdrew her hand. Their eyes met. Her silence was her response.

I am grateful for your company this evening, he said. He handed her a business card. *I will be pleased if our paths cross again.*

She pocketed the card. *Thank you for indulging me,* she said, and leaned in to kiss his cheek before turning to walk away. She liked the scent of him. The not too rough late day stubble along the jawline. She might have turned back, but she didn't. No, not yet, cautioned the inner voice of reason. The voice that counters confusion. And, despair.

Saturday, she admired the early works of Paul Klee in a small museum near the hotel. She trailed a guided tour of the city's historic architecture and then stood at the railing on a tour boat gazing across the expansive lake to snow-covered mountain peaks.

Afterward, she sat on a bench at a lakeside square watching two casually dressed men play chess with nearly human-sized pieces on a board painted onto the pavement. Occasionally, one or the other squatted briefly to study the board before the next move. Cigarettes dangled from their lips, which they dropped, one after another, into a pail of sand after lighting the next from the embers. They never spoke to each other, not once, nor to anyone else. They may not have even known each other.

Day turned to night. At the hotel bar, she stopped for a light bite to eat. She sat at a high top table with a plate of mixed cheeses, which she slipped, slice after slice, onto chunks of crusty bread and washed down with a tall glass of dark beer. She watched strangers and lovers at the bar sidle up to each other for warmth, as artificially intimate as the chess players. As dinner with a stranger. Anonymous encounters all.

When she arrived at the airport the next morning, she felt the man's business card still in her jacket pocket, which she tossed, without a glance, before she boarded the plane. She had no need to know his name.

The Chemistry Professor's Wife

When the chemistry professor acknowledged what became infamous on campus as the hot pad incident, he claimed his marriage had blown up over his wife's electric heating pad.

A bloody hot pad, he grumbled.

Jonathan is not British. He spent a semester at Cambridge twenty years ago and at rare moments when words fail him, he resorts to hyperbolic Anglo jargon. *Bollocks* and *brilliant* are his favorites.

When asked to elaborate on the hot pad episode, or his marriage, he deftly evades explanation by pontificating instead on the euphemistic cliché.

Relationships, the chemistry of the romantic, he says, *are more effectively likened to dynamic chemicals streamed into a beaker only to produce a static substance.*

Chemistry is Jonathan's sole frame of reference, as if everything and everyone might be explained by compounding. Inscribed on a plaque on his desk, and on the classroom blackboard, are his words to live by: *everything is chemistry and chemistry is everything.*

The truth is, I too am not qualified to assess relationships. A thirty-seven year-old graduate student with three master's degrees, I've never cohabitated for more than a few months. I'm a snob and a perfectionist, also a romantic: an untenable combination. I've switched fields of study from biology to sociology to eastern philosophy, where I think I've landed, although one never knows. At present, I'm a PhD candidate and, like Jonathan and his wife, Gwen, reside on campus, supplementing my income by working at the college library where the decorous ambiance and abundance of reading material satisfy my cerebral disposition.

Gwen was a rare friend that year. My first year on campus, her last. I noticed her at once, ensconced from early morning well into afternoons at a library carrel way in back, barely visible behind a pile of books she read with nearly evangelical zeal. She stopped frequently to scribble in one of several Moleskin journals, all with a gold number decal on the cover, to keep track, I supposed. She greeted me with a warm smile each morning when the doors opened and we began the day with the usual small talk. After a time, when I insisted she take a break when I took my break, I escorted her to the lower level café for tea. She said she appreciated the respite because she often has to be shaken out of immersion. I'm the same. There we conversed on more erudite topics from genetics to linguistics and I began to suggest alternative, you might say unorthodox reading material, which, I believe, was implicated in her departure.

I recently overheard students in a science study group compare the hot pad incident to spontaneous combustion and I couldn't help but counter that whatever is incendiary requires fuel. However, it is true, the marriage essentially ceased to exist the moment the heating pad ceased to function. Not so much cause and effect as correlation.

As the story goes, Jonathan was sprawled on the sofa that night because his back had spasmed so badly he had to give up marking exams. Tall and narrow, like a human test tube, he filled the length of the couch, pressed head to socked toes between the armrests. Moments later, while attempting to resuscitate the heating pad, Gwen said he bounced around like a hyperactive child, nothing like his typically professorial demeanor.

He seemed miraculously pain free, she said.

Adrenaline is known to suppress pain, I suggested.

What's wrong with this thing? Jonathan groused that night while banging on the pad and clicking the on-off switch again and again like a child punching elevator buttons. Finally he stood to unplug, examine the plug, re-plug and then wiggle the plug with such ferocity Gwen said she had to stifle a scream. After one last toggle of the switch, he pitched the pad to the floor, where it lay listless and superfluous like a stuffed bear rejected by a toddler.

Gwen froze, holding a teapot of freshly brewed chamomile tea in hand and a plate of warm oatmeal cookies on the kitchen counter. The scent of cinnamon should have warmed her, she said, had she not felt a freeze settle over her heart, as if a microscopic layer of ice had descended over the room, putting a halt to the natural order, just as the hyacinth and bluebells in the flowerbeds bordering the library were stymied last spring by a rare late frost.

Gwen is the last person on earth I can imagine cold. She is the embodiment, in spirit, of a fresh home-baked cookie – crunchy to the teeth and sweet on the tongue. Long and lean, she was the tall girl at the tail of the line of classmates and in adolescence the tormented target of shorter boys. She said when she first met Jonathan, she liked looking up to him. He reminded her of Harry Potter. We were both fans of the series and referenced characters as if family. Jonathan, I would imagine doesn't have a magical bone in his body, nor tolerance for the supernatural. He prefers comparison to Albert Einstein, his idol, as he too wears thick glasses and has dark hair like a halo of bristle. I'm certain Jonathan also expects to win a Nobel Prize.

With wide eyes, a long oval face, and skin as pale as parchment, Gwen could be mistaken for the poet Emily Dickinson. She too has hair more orange than red, like the flares of a hearth fire, suggesting a fiercer nature than evident.

No, you cannot judge a book by its cover, the shy Gwen once told me, what I'm sure she's said many times over the years to contradict the classic image of a fiery redhead.

She didn't have to explain. I knew from the first she was a gentle soul. I also suspected a sleeping dragon within. She told me her feminist mother inspired her independent streak, but it was her father who had the greater influence. A bookworm and classical music-lover, he was the parent who advised her to read Margaret Mead and Ruth Benedict, as well as the great poets. Gwen subsequently earned a master's in cultural anthropology.

Despite Jonathan's urging, however, and her mother's counsel, she resisted an advanced degree because, she said, she was certain she hadn't the wherewithal to tackle the research or contend with the onerous demands of academia. *I wish I were so rational.*

The night Jonathan waged battle with the heating pad, he was wearing one of a selection of white cotton T-shirts he wears on campus, tucked into pressed jeans, and sporting a casual jacket, charcoal or navy, as a rule, never buttoned, in an effort to appear more like a Silicon Valley wunderkind than a professor. The T-shirts display wry science-geek sayings like *Descartes, therefore I am,* or *Never Trust an Atom, They Make Up Everything,* or the one he was wearing the night I met him, a line drawing of a partially filled beaker, with the caption, *If you're not part of the solution, you're part of the precipitate.*

Gwen said the sofa where he rested was the sofa they acquired from a thrift shop when they first moved into their faculty apartment eight years ago. The fabric had faded and the cushions deflated, but neither believed in change for the sake of change. Beyond an overflowing book collection, all was just as it was when they first settled into the bright spacious flat on the top floor of one of six three-story buildings at the edge of the graceful campus, a short walk down a tree-lined path to classrooms and far enough from dormitories to escape blaring music and late night drunken caterwauling. On occasion, a train whistle can be heard in the distance, which charmed Gwen but bothered Jonathan late at night.

These days, the train whistle stirs in me an intense yearning. A Doctor Zhivago sort of nostalgia.

Gwen told me she was delighted with the apartment after two years in a cramped studio in Oakland, while Jonathan completed his dissertation research and she taught rudimentary anthropology at a secondary school for overachieving students. Gwen had attended the sprawling UCLA, and Jonathan Berkeley, so when he completed his degree and accepted a tenure-track assistant professorship at this small North Carolina college, a post relinquished by a prestigious chemist, she appreciated the landscape, as I do: the trees regal and voluminous, the sky often blindingly blue, the subtle fragrance of spruce and pine.

I reside in a duplicate one-bedroom apartment in Building #6 with the same thick coats of paint on the walls and planked floors refinished to a maple glow. However the prize of their place, not mine, sadly, is a glass-enclosed porch set up as a home office, outfitted with a wide and deep oak desk with three drawers on either side, suitable for sharing.

The previous tenants left a tall bookcase that fills the one wall, Gwen told me. *It's painted federal blue, so in the early morning, the light reflects off the bookcase to the floor as if waves to the sand.* She shrugged, embarrassed by her enthusiasm for a porch. I was charmed.

Soon after they arrived on campus, Gwen took a position proofreading anthropology department publications. She spent most mornings, sometimes afternoons, working at the desk on the porch. With a southern exposure and shaded by deciduous trees, the space is comfortably cool in summer and warm enough in spring and fall, but when the cold set in, or on damp days, she used the heating pad like a lap blanket.

I tend to lose track of time there, she confided. *The quiet, the seclusion, comes over me like a warm breeze, and sometimes I just sit watching students frolicking on the back lawn or the last autumn leaves drift from the trees.*

I told her she was a poet at heart and she shook her head no. Gwen never imagined herself as quixotic as she was.

Since they arrived on campus, Jonathan became as renowned as his predecessor for his research into chemical analogs and Gwen felt the need one day to explain his field of study. I was familiar with the science, of course, but I would never deny her the pleasure of serving as translator.

An analog is a chemical compound structurally similar to another with the exception of one singular component, and that component will make the substance behave differently, she pronounced proudly, as if Jonathan had discovered gravity.

Humans can be an analog as well, I remember thinking. We are made of the same basic biochemical composition and with similar proclivities, however doomed, too often, to loneliness because of one critical incompatibility. Most humans, in my experience, do not recognize the dissonance, until the damage is done.

I had noticed Jonathan around campus, but we were formally introduced just once, at a faculty gathering. I was curious about him, having not yet met anyone right enough for me. And from what Gwen had told me, I could not imagine why she chose him. Surely she was taken by his brainpower. I get it. Most women, I have found, tend to stop at one presiding attraction, assuming all else will fall into place and, too often, there is nothing else.

The night we met, Jonathan had a glass of red wine in one hand, his other arm draped around Gwen's shoulder like an armrest. He said he was happy to meet his wife's new friend, the way a parent might speak of a child's playmate at school. When I commented on her broad interests and range of reading, he nodded, but with an officious smirk, as if her impressive intellect might be rare in a woman.

I might have taken offense at the comment, but I had already formed an opinion of the professor. Patronizing, absolutely, bordering on insufferable, but I don't think he means to offend. Men of science are caught up at best in the trees or, like Jonathan, at the root. The forest is beyond their ken and the laboratory their ecosystem.

If I were to describe Gwen, I would say her face lights up when she's fascinated. I would say she prizes discovery; she doesn't hypothesize or predict outcomes, the way scientists do. I would say she is far more divine than pragmatic and infinitely more discerning than the professor, no matter his genius IQ.

Yes, I fell madly in love with Gwen, despite our differing orientation. The heart has no reason and logic has no place in affairs of the heart. You might say we were analog, and not my first unrequited love. I have at times seduced a straight woman to my bed, an egoistic pleasure for me and sometimes an awakening for her, but not Gwen. I'm no fool. Beyond being drawn to her, I felt from the first she needed more than a friend, or a lover – she needed a champion, which the chemistry professor was decidedly not.

Gwen once disclosed that Jonathan captivated her early in their courtship with a late night pontification on the complexities of stability, reactivity, toxicity and, ironically, flammability: the foundations of chemical connections and corrections he defined as the path to equilibrium. Gwen had accepted without question he knew more than she, although she believed equilibrium to be a matter of balance, a lesson first derived from the heating pad. She spoke of it like a cherished companion – a plastic pad the size of a placemat, clothed in the original emerald-green cotton, softened and faded by repeated washings. On the switch, there were three settings: the low subtle and the high nearly scorching. Only the medium setting delivered sustained therapeutic heat.

I suffered chronic stomachaches when I was a girl, she explained. *Stress, I suppose. I was always a bit anxious. There never seemed a better explanation. When I was in pain, my father told me to lay still with the heating pad over my belly and visualize something beautiful, like butterflies or beaches. I suppose it was an introduction to meditation, although he never described it as such. I remember feeling better the moment I heard the click of the control switch – a resounding promise of comfort. Know what I mean? When I asked what medium means, I remember his answer verbatim. He said medium is not hot and not cold. Not high or low. Medium is equidistance, a balance, like the center axis on a seesaw.* She smiled, nostalgically. *I loved the seesaw.*

The idea of middle ground, the relative position between extremes, loomed large for young Gwen and in fourth grade she wrote and illustrated a story about a modest tree in a dense forest that was always looking up to the taller older trees or down at the fledglings, certain only of its existence by comparison. She said the teacher pinned her story on the honor wall and told Gwen's parents it was a sophisticated study in contrast.

That was a surprise, she said, *because what I meant to express, although I had no word for it then, was harmony.* She paused in thought and then added, *I once told Jonathan about my father's interpretation of medium and he said what my dad described was median, not medium.*

Seriously? I asked, unable to veil my contempt.

Seriously, she answered, with a gracious smile, and then she sighed, a sigh so deep I felt the immensity of her disenchantment even more than I presumed and more than I believe she acknowledged to herself.

Once Jonathan and Gwen settled into campus life, she said they seemed to track in tandem. He earned tenure in record time, that factoid is posted on his faculty page on the university website, and soon after, while preparing to publish, he pronounced to Gwen it was time to start a family.

I was shocked, she said. *You see, we had from the first agreed that children were not essential. Jonathan has never shown any interest in kids, not his brother's kids or any others. He's hardly a coddler.*

I had to restrain a guffaw at that remark.

And the other thing is, I know this may sound strange, but he brought it up after dinner, as if an afterthought, and also, in effect, a foregone conclusion. We were washing the dishes. I would wash and he would dry, you see, that was the routine, because we prefer to start each new day without the vestiges of the day before. I asked him why he wanted children and he was quite logical about it. We were the right age, he said. We were more financially secure because of tenure. He assumed, because I had no plans to pursue graduate study, I had plenty of time on my hands. And then he spoke of destiny.

Destiny? Hardly a scientific term.

Not providence. Genetic destiny. Darwinian. The perpetuation of the species. Not exactly family planning. She paused, embarrassed by her sarcasm, so rarely voiced.

What did you say to this?

I said children were hard on a budget. I wanted more time and money to build a nest egg and to travel. I brought up over-population and the equalization of global resources. We all need to play a part in moderating demand, right? Balancing the ecosystem? He was incredulous, and thoroughly exasperated, and when he asked if I didn't want children at all, the argument broke down.

Gwen, as it turns out, never wanted children, and she believed Jonathan was of the same mind. She told me she suspected from childhood that mothering was not for her. She'd had little interest in dolls; she favored puzzles and books. As an adolescent, instead of babysitting, she walked dogs to earn spare cash. More to the point, she said she did not feel up to the task, the responsibility, of another life. I get that too. When she was fifteen, when everything she had read, everything in the media and everything other girls talked about presumed that women, even feminist women, would have families, she asked her mother if something was wrong with her.

Absolutely nothing is wrong with you, her mother answered. *Not every woman is meant to be a mother. All that matters is that children are a choice. Smart women make smart choices.*

There were several subsequent debates about having a child, between which Gwen said Jonathan avoided her like a toxic substance. She ultimately came to the realization that for him, his entire existence, which included a family, was the personal equivalent of advancing through the scientific method.

In the end, she relented.

I may not have chosen to have a child, but I chose my husband and compromises must be made, she said, without a trace of irony or regret.

To my mind, there is a thin line, extremely thin, between compromise and concession.

Jonathan was nearly giddy with her decision, Gwen reported. Their enthusiasm waned however when she lost the first pregnancy, and then three more. Persistent miscarriage. Each time, after the searing pain and bleeding, with barely a nod to the loss, Gwen lay in bed with the heating pad pressed over the womb, soothing body and spirit and hoping to dismiss a disturbing conviction that her resistance to having children was to blame, as if she had manifested failure.

Three years passed until a specialist detected a rare chromosomal abnormality that negates sustainability of a fetus. Such anomalies do not affect either partner alone, but in combination prevent a pregnancy from ever taking hold.

The man of science was flummoxed and Gwen overheard him describe to his parents what he framed as a biological impasse. He said he could not believe he married the one woman in a million who turned out to be an organic mismatch.

In the weeks and months following, Jonathan was as solicitous as possible, which Gwen appreciated, but then he focused on publishing another book, after which he spent a summer lecturing at symposiums across the country. He has published many articles since in prestigious journals and co-authored multiple grants to fund university research. These days, he's frequently trotted out to donor events to secure capital funding for a new science wing.

Not long before we met, Gwen's father was diagnosed with pancreatic cancer and she returned home. She took the heating pad with her and said her dad had tears in his eyes when she ceremonially plugged it in, pressed medium, and told him to picture butterflies or beaches.

Although her mother made arrangements to work from home, she was often called to meetings at the educational foundation where she served as executive director. Gwen steeped soups and smoothies. She read aloud her father's favorite poetry. They created classical music playlists. She played scrabble with him through sleepless nights and it was during one of those marathon games, at the word harbinger, that she confessed her concern she might have inadvertently sabotaged her pregnancies.

You know better, her father said. *Not like you to think that way. However, my sweet girl, this may be the time to give serious consideration to what you want, rather than what you don't want.*

His words weighed heavily on her mind. After he died, she returned to campus with his favorite CDs, a box of family photos and the heating pad. She took on additional editing work and when Jonathan again suggested graduate study, she baulked.

I told him he'd have to accept a lesser wife and he didn't argue the point. He rarely argues much anymore. He's lost his taste for debate, at least with me.

Gwen had accepted she was no longer a worthy partner – neither professor nor graduate student, nor progenitor of the species, she lost her balance and lost a sense of destiny separate from his. This broke my heart.

Even though Jonathan was rarely home the last year, Gwen decided to spend her mornings at the library, carving out space, I suspect, not contaminated by his gloomy disposition. She reread Margaret Mead, and her partner, Gregory Bateson, and then the contemporary ethnography they've inspired. She devoured a new text on symbolic anthropology, a subset of the field exploring rituals and symbols as a way of defining cultures. I recommended titles I hoped might get her back in touch with her youthful equilibrium. The journals of introspective thinkers like Annie Dillard and May Sarton. Travel essays by Rebecca West. I also suggested readings on Buddhism,

mysticism and the existential search for meaning –
eternal fascination for me that I hoped would provide a
missing link for Gwen.

At first, when I piled these musty tomes on the
desk, she smiled with an expression of forbearance. I'm
certain she perused them only to be kind. Before long,
however, she was engrossed for days in a large leather-
bound illustrated volume on chakras with an elaborate
gilded cover and thick paper. Nearly biblical.

Indian philosophy delineates the seven chakras
as the foundation for physical and emotional harmony,
and each chapter featured watercolor drawings of their
symbols with the accompanying mythological and
medicinal anecdotes.

After she read and re-read that book, Gwen
often seemed lost in thought. She doodled images of
chakras in her journal. She composed a list of the
happy thoughts she had called to mind when she was a
sickly child resting with the heating pad, beyond
beaches and butterflies: Redwoods, the nightly call of
crickets and katydids, the crunch underfoot on the first
blanket of autumn leaves. A steady stream of tears
dripped down her cheeks. I pretended not to notice. A
week later, she listed names for her unborn babies:
Drew, Dylan, Finn and Riley. Again I watched her weep
and this time, I wept with her.

I'm sure she never mentioned the readings or
writings to Jonathan. No reason to share with the
chemistry professor such deeply personal introspection,
or a melancholy for what was lost, as the chemistry
professor was focused on the future.

The last time I saw Gwen, the day she left behind her journals for safekeeping, or as a parting gift, I'll never be sure, she told me she had awakened early that morning, before her husband's alarm announced the day. She slipped out of bed and stood for a moment in the doorway watching him sleep.

In the early morning light, he seems pristine, she said. *I wonder what chemical magic he makes in his dreams? What natural wrongs of the natural world he hopes to right?*

The chemist is concerned with repair, not renewal, I remarked.

Gwen nodded. *The chemist pours himself a half-glass and spends a lifetime replicating the full.*

I'm certain she didn't mean to turn so cold the night Jonathan attempted to pummel the dysfunctional heating pad into submission. She knew the device had outlived its use and would have to be replaced. But as he pounded on the pad, she feared she too might shut down, or explode, such extremes the antithesis to equilibrium.

Jonathan insisted everything is eventually replaced by something better. *The heating pad itself succeeded the hot water bottle, right?* he argued.

Sobbing, Gwen bent to retrieve the heating pad, rolled it into a cylinder, wrapped the chord around it and secured the ends with a knot, as she had countless times before, and then, cradling the pad in her arms like an infant, she buried it on an upper shelf of the bedroom closet behind spare blankets and a shoebox filled with photos.

Jonathan was briefly speechless. He had rarely seen his wife cry. He promised a new heating pad and, true to his word, returned the next day with a replacement – a black mesh liner with a gel insert to be heated in the microwave or frozen as a cold pack. The pad required no wires, no switch.

A hot-cold pad for the modern age, he pronounced proudly.

Gwen saw at once, what Jonathan failed to see: the heat would start too hot, or not hot enough, and steadily dissipate. No sustained warmth. No balance.

The next night, Jonathan attended a faculty gathering at the library. Gwen declined, complaining of a sour stomach. What I knew, and he didn't, is that earlier that day, she was reading about the third chakra with an expression of near rapture on her face. The Manipura, as it is known, located in the abdomen and represented by the color yellow, personifies fire and signifies transformation.

Perhaps, Gwen noted in her journal, this chakra is the source of the expression, *a fire in the belly.*

I was in attendance that evening, wondering where Gwen was and standing with a group of professors discussing curriculum politics when we heard sirens approaching the campus. Conversation came to a halt, in that way people stop in their tracks at the premonition of disaster, and when the sirens passed the library and continued toward the residences, an architecture professor said, *sounds like they're headed to faculty housing. No surprise. Those older buildings, the circuitry is no longer up to code.*

When the fire trucks stopped at the edge of campus, as suspected, I had the crazy thought the fire had something to do with the hot pad, and the fright on Jonathan's face suggested he thought the same. He must have been furious, but on those rare occasions when he spoke of the incident, he maintained his wife was not to blame. Instead, he insisted, she was merely foolish, ignorant, he argued, in his own defense, of the science behind thermal energy.

Jonathan knows better. Fire is not a compound. Fire is not an element or a substance. Fire is an exothermic chemical reaction producing heat both incandescent and fluorescent, like the surface of the sun, its rays as restorative as deadly and as incongruous as an eternally sleeping dragon.

I will forever imagine Gwen that night, prone on the sofa with the heating pad plugged in and spread over her midline chakra. She might have been contemplating the Zen reverence for heat – the essential spark for transformation – as in the alchemy of gold from metals, the modulation of mind over matter. Sheathed in the imagined warmth of the heating pad, and childhood memory, she may have closed her eyes to conjure images of beaches or butterflies.

She would have been unaware of the spark of a short circuit. Before long, smoke would have seared her nose and throat and snaked into her lungs, yet she would have remained immobile, in a dream-like state, one hand on her belly, the other over her heart.

Her eyes may have fluttered open when she heard the sirens. She would have seen flames creeping from the electrical socket up the wall and tiny flares slithering along the ceiling molding like the tongue of a mythological dragon. Slowly, with tremendous effort, I picture her rousing her beleaguered body. Perhaps she stood several seconds in place, her legs heavy, lungs heaving, and then, as if summoned from another world, with a determination she never imagined she had, she would have made her way to the door, out of the apartment and down the stairs, fleeing life-threatening flames and smoke, and a dispassionate marriage, into the cool night air, where she might breathe again.

A White Writer

As I approached the table toward the rear of the slick downtown restaurant my lunch companion had reserved, he stood and reached for my hand with a wide-eyed expression of surprise.

I was convinced you were brown, he said.

I was too startled by the comment to respond, so I held his gaze instead and then stretched out my hand to meet his with a sturdy shake.

Thank you, I murmured, as I slipped into the leather-backed chair he pulled out for me. My voice sounded tentative, far more than usual and less self-assured than I hoped to appear. I had planned to be appropriately deferential, not meek.

I might have mentioned he surprised me as well – taller than expected, also bulkier, a barrel chest only partially hidden by an elegant brown suede sport jacket, worn open over a crisp white shirt unbuttoned at the neck to reveal a nest of gray chest hair. At his temples, gray patches of hair contrasted sharply with a tightly trimmed dark brown clipper-cut.

Do you not lunch with white women? I asked.

He smiled, not sheepishly, rather proudly. *I cannot remember the last time.*

Other than the color of his skin, which, in the photograph on the magazine website, seemed darker than the mocha it was, he bore little resemblance to his image. Must have been an older photo, perhaps staged to appear younger and more dignified to reinforce the austerity of his position as a founding editor and principal culture critic of a prestigious journal for black readers. Little had been divulged in his bio beyond journalism awards, mention of his upbringing in Missouri, the eldest of nine children, that speaks volumes about personality, and a commendation he received from Barack Obama for service to both presidential campaigns. He seemed otherwise to reside in a vacuum, his work his identity and his identity his work. In this, we were the same.

I crossed one leg over the other and pulled the hem of my dress over that knee, settling into a formal meeting pose, and when I looked up, he was watching me, scrutinizing me, I would say, although his dappled complexion and a broad gap-toothed smile suggested benevolence, even as nearly black eyes floated ruthlessly on clouds of white.

Steady, I cautioned myself. This distinguished media critic is, as expected, imposing, but intimidating only if permitted.

What made you think I was brown? I asked.

The headshot on your website. Sort of sepia, hard to be sure.

Couldn't we all be hybrids? I answered, sitting as tall and straight as possible. I am not a tall woman, so I've learned to compensate with bold body language.

Hybrid? Only a Caucasian would use that term.

Literal. You subscribe to the one-drop rule?

Optimistically, yes, but not you, I suspect.

One can never be sure. I should take that DNA test that's so popular these days. You know, to trace family roots? I hear it can be a revelation.

He observed me in that way men assess women through a narrow lens and, in this case, with clearly perceived antipathy. Was it color or gender, or both?

A waitress approached the table to take drink orders. A petite perky blonde, her gold hoop earrings shimmered under low-hanging chandeliers. A student, I presumed, perhaps an aspiring actress, and I couldn't help but wonder whom she went home to or what sort of demons she lives with, my mind forever searching for the story. She stood by his chair and looked to him to place the order, but he extended his palm toward me.

Just water for me now, please, a tall one, no ice, with lemon, I requested.

When the waitress started to ask about which type of water, he interrupted. *Bring a bottle of mineral water and ice for me.* She nodded and left, summarily dismissed.

So, he said. *I'm not one for small talk, even agenda-centered small talk. Let's cut to the chase, shall we? Why does a white woman, of European origin, I suspect...*

Second generation, I interjected.

Okay, a second-generation American with dark eyes and hair and, I see now, olive skin. Mediterranean descent, no doubt. Why would that woman write a novel about race in America?

That question itself is merely further evidence of the divide, don't you think?

I don't need evidence, he retorted.

I stiffened at the rebuke. I would have to speak more strategically. I was on tenuous ground here.

No one challenges a male writer who writes female characters. No one asks a straight novelist how he or she writes gay, or visa versa. I would imagine no one asked Alice Walker how or why she featured a white freedom rider in her first novel, Meridian. You know it?

Of course.

A Northeast Jew, as I recall, in thrall to a sixties style of idealism, depicted as unequivocally self-serving, not at all flattering to the white women of that period who stepped into the line of fire for civil rights. No one took Walker to task.

I was quite taken with that novel and I reviewed it last year at the forty-year mark of the magazine...

Yes, I read that piece. The defining literature.

He nodded, obviously pleased. *So why would anyone take Alice Walker to task? She presented an honest characterization. And we all knew from the first she was a writer to reckon with.*

Ah, the first direct hit. Apparently I was not such a writer. I sat back in my chair, but not wanting to appear deflated, I leaned forward again and crooked an elbow on the table, cupping my jaw with that hand as if merely sharing an anecdote with a friend.

I heard her speak recently. Brilliant. Wonderful smile. Although she is one angry woman.

Angrier with age, bless her heart. We require angry black women.

Another waiter, second team, scrawny and brown, brought two glasses and poured water from a large green bottle, which he left on the table. I caught his eye and smiled, because wait staff tend to be invisible, and he returned the smile, but then vanished quickly. I imagine he had been cautioned against any fraternizing with the clientele. Another divide.

My companion seized the moment to scan the lunch menu, so I followed his lead. The bistro was bustling now – loud voices, feigned laughter. Business relationships cemented, deals underway. Urban lunch the means to very specific ends.

When the waitress returned, we ordered. She quizzed us on every possible variable – with or without cheese, salads tossed or dressing on the side, meat or fish cooked to what temperature, and so on – listening as attentively as if we were dictating an amendment to the constitution. She entered the information into a handheld electronic tablet, responding to each answer with one word: *perfect*. I noticed out of the corner of my eye the critic stifled a smile.

So you too have noticed that every server these days seems to think everything is positively perfect, I said after she left.

And sales clerks. Service representatives. Even the cook at my favorite food truck.

I chuckled. So the critic had a sense of humor. Promising.

The busboy returned with a basket of bread, which the critic waved away. It was rude not to offer me the option, arrogance apparently suited to the persona. I was hungry, but held my tongue.

He gazed at me again, more appreciably. Might have been my eyes. In daylight they appear green, in lower light, blue, presiding over prominent cheekbones, a sculpted jaw and long neck, a little like a Modigliani. Shoulder length brown hair is streaked heavily now with silver strands, which I hope hints at distinguished writers like Joan Didion and Susan Sontag. I wore a knit wrap dress, in russet tweed, which suits my skin tone, with a deep V-neck, slimming to hips spreading with age and a sedentary lifestyle. At the last minute, I put on a pair of dangling silver earrings and dark green-rimmed glasses, what my current man-friend calls the sexy librarian look. Any port in a storm, I thought, as I dabbed jasmine body oil down my décolletage, before I ran out of the house to make sure to arrive on time.

The critic had no notebook, nor a recording device, unless he planned to use his phone, which sat on the table just under one hand as if a grenade, and I grew increasingly apprehensive he would use the meeting not for the interview I was expecting, but to decide if there would be an interview. Or worse, to condemn my work. My heart sank a bit, even as I made another effort to counter his opening salvo.

What about Christians writing about the Holocaust? Or a Jew who wasn't there? If you follow your logic, no one can possibly describe an experience without living it. What about John Irving writing a transgender character? The presiding question is, do you have to be one to write one?

Irving has lost his mojo, but that's neither here nor there. Race is not religion or sexual identity. As you said in the book, an insightful comment, by the way – you can hide religion, sexuality or personality, but color, no. The first thing anyone sees and as such, expectations instantly set in stone. Second class, at best.

At least he had read the novel carefully enough to paraphrase. *I'd like a glass of wine,* I said. *Do you mind?*

He waved the waitress over.

A glass of the house red, I requested.

Got it, the girl answered. *And something for you, Sir?*

Bring us a bottle of this syrah, two glasses, he said, pointing to a wine list on a table display card.

Perfect, the waitress responded, and this time we both laughed as she walked away.

Kind of you, I said. *I rarely drink more than one at lunch. Ruins my afternoon. I'm on deadline.*

Aren't we all? I prefer a bottle. It's on the magazine.

Lovely. Must be nice to have an expense account. And no push back? I mean, given my skin tone.

On the lunch? My discretion.

And on the review?

Also my discretion, he said, non-committal and without any sign of magnanimity in his eyes.

My heart ached, a genuine ache; a sensation I often feel, but rarely reveal, of expecting the worst, despite a lifetime of hoping for the best. Regularly resisting the excruciating sensation of being out of control, a chronic condition for all writers – stature, finances, personal lives subject to agents and editors, and the influence of critics, like this one.

What's the deadline? he asked.

An article on older women traveling alone.

Do you sell a lot of those?

Enough to keep me in table wine when the teaching stipend runs out.

Writing fiction as well? Something new?

Yes.

Admirable. Something else meant to shake things up?

True Colors was a character study, hopefully a compelling story. Not a call to action.

That sort of novel always has a purpose, he said.

What sort of novel do you mean?

As much or more between the lines.

All good fiction is between the lines. If there had been a purpose, it would be to stimulate dialogue among white readers – I mean, let's face it, it's white people who need to step up.

I was surprised when he didn't respond to that comment. I wasn't sure if he had already lost interest or was offended. I knew I'd have to argue more eloquently with this man. He's heard it all, no doubt.

He sat back in his chair, so I sat back to equalize the exchange, browsing my memory for an analogy. Storytelling has always been my best defense.

I had an orchid once, a gift, but I've no green thumb.

I leaned forward again to regain command of the conversation and saw the surprise on his face at the abrupt change of subject.

They need tender loving care, I'm told, he remarked.

Yes, by reputation, they are delicate. And, once settled, they don't much like change.

Like most humans I know.

Oh yes, such sensitive creatures we are.

He smiled. *I might say neurotic.*

I nodded affirmatively and took a sip of water.

I found what I thought was a perfect spot, neither too bright nor too dark, cool at night, warm by day. Instead of watering, I put an ice cube at the base, as instructed, every week. I tried to remember to feed regularly. At first, the orchid bloomed beautifully. A gorgeous violet, rainbow violet. Lots of new shoots. I confess, I felt rather righteous.

He listened, without any readable expression, but he was listening.

Before long, the flowers dried and dropped, the leaves spotted and turned brown, and even with absurdly expensive orchid food, nothing happened. Dormant, I hoped. I waited, believing it might miraculously revive, and just when I was about to give up, I noticed a florist with an orchid window display and stepped inside for advice. An older woman at the counter, as wiry and elegant as an orchid, wore a floral scarf wrapped around her head and nodded knowingly at my commentary, like a sage. The sort of woman who wears her entire life history on her face. Know the type?

I do.

She listened to my description in its entirety and when at last she spoke, she smiled, reassuringly, and she had a sultry voice, honestly, the personification of an orchid. I was willing to accept whatever she said.

I know that type as well, he said with a smile.

Here's what she told me. Orchids, like people, have to be shaken up now and then. Not at all what I expected to hear. They need to be uncomfortable for a time in order to re-energize from within. Especially when gripped by inertia, her word. Sort of like people who self-isolate, seeking distance from the general chaos of living.

I could have said that I'm the same – frequently absorbed so completely in reading and writing, I come up for air only when gasping for breath.

The waitress arrived at that moment with the wine and went through the ceremony of presenting the label before uncorking and pouring a taste. The critic went through the motions of sniffing and tasting, and then nodded his satisfaction. She poured a few ounces into each of our glasses and stood the bottle on the table with a napkin wrapped around its neck, smiling as proudly as if she had personally harvested the grapes, before she discretely faded away.

He swirled his wine glass. *The philosopher in the flower shop,* he said, without drinking, so I too waited, the two of us gripping the stems of wine glasses, inches separating us, but without contact, without connection, manifesting, in effect, two hundred years of racial conflict.

I broke the silence. *I was totally surprised by her direction, assuming, as we do, that orchids are hypersensitive.*

Were there more specific instructions?

Oh yes, very specific. She told me to move the orchid. One exposure to another or darker to lighter, she said. Very little water and withhold food. Let it starve a while, she said. Those were the guidelines. And even though counterintuitive, I had nothing to lose, so I shifted the orchid from the study facing east to a kitchen window facing south. I opened the window a touch at the bottom to let in the cool night air. The poor plant had to suffer the indignity of direct sun through the day and shiver through the night.

And?

For one month, no change. The orchid was absolutely naked, comatose, and I concluded the old lady was daft. Then one morning, half asleep, about to grind my caffeine beans, I glanced at the windowsill and there it was: a bud. And soon a new leaf emerged, a perfect green leaf.

Perfect, he mimicked the waitress.

In that case, yes. Perfect. I fed and watered and a week later put the plant back in the original spot, a lovely accent to my work space, and because I still thought indirect light was optimal, and it thrives there to this day.

This relates to your novel how?

We need to shake things up, not just for the sake of it, too much of that going on, but to effect change. We, at least most of us, would agree that racism is rampant and change essential, but nothing will change until we alter our way of thinking about what we've incorporated into our collective narrative. How else will we ever let go of deeply assimilated perceptions of reality? And, I repeat, it's white people who have to change.

When he began to respond, I surprised us both by raising my palm in protest.

Perhaps you will agree we are well beyond new laws, beyond affirmative action or policing policies or education reform. This is about every one of us taking responsibility, all of us having a place in this story.

This story?

Race relations in America. The defining story of this country. Past, present, and future, especially now, as we move into a brown world. Generations of mixed marriages. Blended children. Brown immigrants. We're not black and white anymore.

My dear, we're always black and white, he held.

He reminded me now of a history professor at university who never smiled and never acknowledged radical thinking, only criticized what we missed. I heaved a loud sigh, which he pretended not to notice. I had no clue how to get through to the critic, but I had to. I was there to secure his interest. Desperate to save my story.

Okay, think of it this way, I entreated. *Every book that has received attention in the last twenty years, not the essayists like Coates and Gay, or a poet like Rankine, I'm talking fiction, including the Pulitzer Prize-winning variety, and every major film for that matter, they all go back to slavery or reconstruction. Occasionally the Harlem Renaissance or the sixties. Otherwise, little is written, not that gets out to the general public, in present tense. Post-Obama. Long past Brown v. Board of Ed. Past civil rights legislation. Now. 2016. A period some people are calling post-racialism, although of course that's a misnomer. A different time, yes, but not for everyone, and not different enough. I'm sure you'll grant me that. Also,*

Toni Morrison said to write the book you want to read. I wrote the book I wanted to read.

He put down his wine glass and sat forward with elbows on the table and arms crossed in front of his chest defensively. Nonetheless, I detected a different expression in his eyes: contemplative, less derisive.

A commendable way of thinking, yes. However, our story, the story of my people, Toni's people, you do not have the right to tell that story. You're not the orchid lady.

She's an observer, a specialist, not one of the species!

Separate but equal?

That's not what I meant.

There was a silent pause between us, awkward and rife with emotion, and I had the thought the entire lunch and the intimation of an interview was a sham. I might have been invited to meet with him to be discredited or chastened, and despite the gnawing in my stomach and the rising hysteria that I had been taken advantage of and he might make the situation worse, I would not go down without a fight.

Mr. Johnson...

Henry, please.

Henry, thanks. True Colors is not a memoir. Not a history. It's a novel. Fiction. Where to my mind, the universal truths emerge. An invention with fact at its heart. And the sole obligation of the novelist is to tell the story with authenticity. In this case, the story happens to feature people of varying shades on the color line, married to lighter or darker shades, and raising brown kids dealing with racism in this century.

As long as the story rings true, it should absolutely not matter who wrote the story.

He seemed dumbfounded for a moment, or, like the professor, preparing to pounce. *Tell me, do you advise your students to write what they know?*

A platitude they have heard too often. I remind them this does not mean to write their own story, unless they're writing a memoir. Rather to write the sounds and scents and colors of the world they have experienced. The people, the places. The fears and hopes. And yes, the injustices they condemn. Faulkner said to write the immortal truths... "love and honor and pity and pride and compassion and sacrifice."

Not a fan, he mumbled, as he lifted the wine glass and tipped it toward me to toast. *Here's to shaking things up.*

We clinked. We sipped. I hoped he didn't notice the glass trembling in my grasp. I could not remember feeling so vulnerable, not in my adult life, because this revered commentator had the power to rescue my novel. A novel that took six years to write and was never intended to be about race but ended up so, and despite a plethora of 5-star reviews on Amazon, a smattering of admiring newspaper reviews and glowing write-ups in the trade press, was headed to obscurity. This man alone could do the impossible – endow a small work of fiction from a mid-list writer, published by a tiny press who has stuck by me since the first of two short story collections, twenty years ago, through two even lesser-known novels. This man could attract the attention of a significant audience of readers. Not to mention the validation. I had sent him the book a year ago and never heard back, so I was thrilled with an invitation to lunch and the possibility of a review.

My last chance to flower.

So you think you get it? he asked.

Get what, exactly?

Get what it means to be black, or brown, in America. Seriously? Based on what?

I took another sip of wine, a blatant stall to gather my thoughts, then I looked up into his eyes as innocently as a child angling for an ice cream.

First, a question. What if Shonda Rhimes were white? She's a marvel. One successful television show after another with casts of every color and type, and race is rarely subtext.

Only a white person would suggest race was rarely subtext. And let's remember, Shonda is black.

Yes, yes, apologies, race is of course subtext.

He shook his head vigorously, his eyes again severe. Unforgiving. He leaned toward me menacingly. *Please. Get this right. Race is context.* He broke the word into two words, *con-text*, his tone of voice raised now to contemptuous.

I took a deep breath in, and slowly out, in order to restrain the impulse to tap into swelling anger. I detested his patronage. No one has that right. White women have our share of anger, I might have said, but I held my hostile rhetoric and continued instead in the controlled tone of voice I use with lazy students who try my patience.

Shonda Rhimes said in an interview that we can write about anything, we just have to get it right. However, in your view, because I am a white woman, I cannot read and study and interview, nor can I possibly imagine or intuit the reality of oppression? I know the black experience is unlike any other, I get that, and certainly there are specific truths exclusive to individuals judged first and foremost by the color of their skin. I get that too. But writers write about all sorts of things. Our only obligation is to get it right.

He stared at me in silent exasperation. With me or with a lifetime of discrimination?

Sara, what made you decide to write this book?

The use of my name made the conversation more intimate, although stealthily so, like a bullfighter sidling up to the bull. Was this a learned instinct to neutralize conflict? An elderly black woman I once interviewed echoed that reality. *A lifetime meant to avoid being the pebble in other people's shoes,* she said.

Why did I write this novel? Good question. It started as a short story, but ended up, as you know, with a variety of characters whose lives intersected through one young woman thrust into the limelight in a desperate moment. Because the protagonist of the original story was a black woman whose white husband left her to fend for herself and her children, she remained the heart of the novel. The other characters revolved around her, as it turned out, and she, and her family, they got under my skin, so to speak. They badgered me to tell the whole story. They seemed to speak to me, and through me, and I lived within them, and they within me, for several years. I'm an observer by nature, as writers are, and I filled in the blanks with obsessive reading and lots of interviews, and then took the leap into invention, as novelists do, but always in the context of what I'd learned about race relations.

He continued to stare with a blank expression. Did he believe I was delusional or dishonest?

Just tell me this, he asked. *I'm curious. When do you recall your first awareness of racial conflict? I'm trying to understand what set the scene for your audacious pen.*

What leapt to mind was the boy who often surfaces in my memory. I was twenty years old, in my last semester at college and a student teacher at a so-called inner city school in New York City, a high school distinguished by disorder and discord. I was taken with my students – their humor and energy, their grit, and their grace in the face of discrimination. I loved them all and fell for one – a senior with penetrating eyes, a gentle heart and wisdom beyond his years. He sought me out in my office, and then we met over a soda at a neighborhood coffee shop, ostensibly to talk about literature. There was a prospect for a scholarship to college and I offered to help with the application. And then he invited me to a party. A mix of black and brown, some of his friends were still in school, others working low wage jobs, having given up on their prospects. I was curious about how they behaved off school grounds and off the streets. I suppose I was enticed by the forbidden – the black and white of it, as well as the rob-the-cradle of it, although I was only two years his elder. I knew I was crossing a professional boundary, but I could not resist his smile, his muscular build and large elegant hands, and yes, his lustrous mahogany skin and thick pink lips. We spent more and more time together, curling up in my tiny apartment watching classic films or reading to each other. We went to movies or dawdled at diners well into the night, and before long we were the first of each other's lovers and the combination of the innocent and the erotic set my pale skin on fire. It was an error in judgment, of course, but I was hooked. By the end of the semester, I came to my senses and called it off. He was graduating and I was moving to Manhattan to launch a writing career. He was furious. He accused me of toying with his affections, alleging our relationship had been a dalliance. No, I insisted. He was special to me and I'd hoped I was to him. Yes, I feared for my future as a teacher, because I always knew I would need a day job to pay the rent. I was never one to shake things up, despite what the critic imagined, and I could have told him this story, if I trusted in his compassion. I had told no one except one good friend and another black lover. On the other hand, that wasn't the first time I felt the tyranny of race.

I was seven, maybe eight. My mother's older sister, the only one of six to move away from New York, lived in Virginia, and every summer we drove down there to visit. My aunt and uncle and cousins all spoke what seemed at the time a foreign tongue, that languid southern drawl. They lived in a house on a tree-lined street and I was raised in an apartment overlooking an alley. And still live in an apartment, only slightly larger, and with a better view, I might have added. *The house was small, mind you, in a neighborhood of houses all built with dark brick, but single story. No neighbors above or below, a novelty to a city girl. There was a backyard with a tree swing and overflowing flowerbeds. Clean and bright and quiet, in the afternoons we walked to the high school pool to hang out and we ate dinners outdoors at a picnic table. So civilized.*

He smiled, he listened, and I was grateful for the power of storytelling, also determined to share the truth in a way he might more than understand – he might approve.

One year my father took a second job and could not drive us the nine hours south, so my mother raided the penny jar and eked out enough to buy tickets to fly the two of us on a propjet. That was in the late sixties and I remember my aunt waiting on the tarmac to greet us, like something out of Casablanca, the movie I mean. A whole other time, right?

He nodded, similarly nostalgic.

Anyway, we were at baggage claim and I had to go to the bathroom, so my aunt pointed toward the restrooms and off I went, but I was stopped cold by the two doors labeled white and colored. I knew nothing of Jim Crow. There were few people of color in the Bronx back then, more Latino. Many languages spoken and an angry divide between Jew and Catholic, but not yet black versus white. I stared at those doors to decipher the code, but gave up and returned to my mother and aunt to ask what it meant. My mother, a high school graduate, was an avid reader, a self-educated woman who answered all my questions directly, to a fault. I won't bother you with her introductory monologue on birth control.

At this, he chuckled.

Much to my aunt's obvious discomfort, Mom launched into a diatribe about the sins of slavery and the civil war, and took my aunt to task that the two doors were still marked differently, as if she personally shouldered the blame. But here's the thing. My mother answered the wrong question. I had heard my father refer to blacks as coloreds, so I knew what that meant. In the naiveté of childhood, I simply did not understand what it meant to be white. After all, none of us are white. I held out one arm, rolled up a sleeve, and pointed to the exposed lower arm. *We are peach toned or beige or tan or some similar shade, not white. And, I must say, when the black power movement designated black as the terminology, I thought the same: who is truly black? Even ebony is a stretch.*

I wished at that moment that I'd incorporated this memory into the novel, because after all these years, I still feel the enormity of this hypocrisy, and having made language my life's work, I know how words are used to misrepresent, inflame and perpetuate inequity.

So, that's what I remember. The simple lack of sense of it. A child inherently recognizes we're all the same and discrimination is imposed by the fearful, the small-minded and malicious. And when I taught high school, I watched kids of color deal with the indignities of racism, including the bias of white teachers. I was outraged, then and still. I know it's not my life, not really my battle, but this cannot stand...

I stopped speaking, nearly panting and nearly in tears, frantic to validate my existence as a writer, but also a human being. All because of one book, a novel read by maybe a few thousand people and headed to bookstore discount tables or for sale for a quarter at library discard shops, and not the first good book to live a short life.

Our salads arrived, a necessary, hopefully brief halt to the conversation. As he took his first bite, I added a postscript. *While I was researching True Colors, I read W. E. B. Du Bois. His philosophy of dual consciousness stopped me cold. His essays clarified the duplicity of racism and that spurred me on with even greater intent. I was determined to get it right.*

The critic put down his fork, took first a sip of water and then a sip of wine. *Du Bois is my hero. He foresaw before the turn of the 19th century, before the industrial revolution, before the great migration, long before Jim Crow, what black people would forever face in this country. On the other hand, he never had to face 21st century social media. African Americans are no longer slaves or, legally, second-class citizens. We are however a threat – cockroaches to be crushed. On NPR the other day, a one hundred year-old black woman said, if you're not at the table, you're the meal. Now that's authenticity!*

He summoned the waitress. *Soufflé today?* he asked. When she nodded, he turned to me with unexpected exuberance to say, *terrific chocolate soufflé here. Shall we?*

Chocolate and wine, my kind of lunch, I answered, hoping the time we waited for the desert would be on my side.

We stopped talking while we ate, muffled by the din of conversation and the clang of utensils.

Hard to eat salad without making noise, isn't it? he asked, as if the previous conversation had never occurred.

I despise men who seamlessly shift from a dialogue they'd rather not have to small talk, or worse: shut down entirely when words are too hard to say. This man, a man of the written word, did not strike me as one to shy away from any debate. In that moment, however, I was worn out by a defensive posture. And starving. Once we finished our salads, he pushed the bowl away, refilled our wine glasses and leaned toward me, glass in hand.

What you've written, Sara. This novel. Daring. Risky. And not disrespectful, I recognized that in the first few pages. Also extremely well crafted. That's the reason the reviews have been good. You should be proud. However, the magazine's mission is to promote black culture and black artists. We're not inclined to review a white writer, no matter the material.

He tipped his glass to me as if an honor had been bestowed and sipped, holding the wine a moment in his mouth with a supremely satisfied expression on his face.

I searched my brain for a persuasive response. *Do I recall correctly that the magazine's subhead says something about enhancing the black experience?*

He nodded, with a knowing smile. *Yes, I know where you're going. We should have come up with black lives matter, that's the magazine's raison d'être.*

And there it was. Sentenced without a trial. I regretted having to wait for the soufflé, wishing I might flee to a safe place to rant, or cry.

On the other hand, he added, *this novel is an important addition to commercial literature on race. I wanted to better understand your motives.*

I would hope the book stands for itself, at least in terms of motivation.

One never knows until one asks, right?

I suppose. Now what?

Now dessert, he answered, brightening at the sight of a slim bronze woman with almond-shaped hazel eyes who could be the model for the new brown race. She approached with a tray holding a steaming white crock and a small matching pitcher, then placed the soufflé on the center of the table before slicing open to reveal a dark molten heart.

Thank you, he said, with a warm smile – a smile I wish he had granted me – and then he silently ladled portions for each of us, dripping the melted chocolate on top.

What do you call this color? I asked.

He chuckled. *You are cheeky.*

I prefer the right words.

He stiffened and put down the spoon, gently so as not to clang, although I heard it loud and clear.

My dear, this is not fiction. This is my world, a world you do not inhabit. Black is black, brown is black. This soufflé is the color of an ancient harvest. Scorched earth and blood. White? White is a billowy cloud on a blue sky. White is snow on Christmas morning. Purity. Superiority. Get it right!

His words, his voice, his pained expression, were the final smack in my face. I had been officially humiliated, and yet, to stay silent seemed a greater indignity.

I follow a few tweeters on racial issues and one posted recently this question: can bi-racial activists represent blacks? With a link to an article I confess is still in my queue. So now we have a new group to ostracize? The color line gets cut ever more fine?

The color line is and has forever been cut fine. I think you know that. You've done your homework. And you've proven to be an empathetic soul. But you are not one of us. And my job is to promote us, every shade on our palette. I only separate out white.

I put down the spoon, the chocolate bitter on my tongue. He savored a few more spoonfuls before wiping the residue from his mouth, his white napkin now streaked dark brown. When he signaled for the check, I hastened to the restroom to gather sufficient courage to walk out of the restaurant with a semblance of self-respect.

I washed my hands and shook them dry while staring into the mirror. Judged, condemned, by the color of my skin. Fitting, I suppose. The white woman with no leverage.

As I returned to the table, he stood and waved me ahead of him through the restaurant to the exit. A bright sky blinded me momentarily as we stood face-to-face on the sidewalk, and when he extended his hand to shake, I took it with both hands and held on so tightly he couldn't easily pull away.

So that's it? I demanded. *The magazine, through you, preserves the divide?*

The divide is the divide.

He stared at me, and I stared back, even as the glare of the afternoon sun burned into my eyes.

Now you are the persecutor. You are the racist.

He jerked his hand from my grasp. *An outrageous accusation!*

If the shoe fits! I couldn't believe these words were coming out of my mouth. *You know, I came of age in the wake of the modern feminist era. Nevertheless, men still rule, men retain the power, especially in the workplace. I know what it means to have doors closed in your face. To be refused to be taken seriously. I don't much like it either. Did you take me to lunch to belittle me? Was this my personal lynching?*

He raised his voice angrily. *You cannot use that word. Not your word, not your history. Why don't you get that?*

I stopped myself from speaking again, ashamed of my outburst.

I do get it. I apologize. Truly. I appreciate the lunch and the opportunity to defend my work, even if dismissed. Just tell me this. I sent the book a year ago. Why now?

You sent me a copy? My assistant manages books that come in over the transom. I choose books to review, as a rule, in consultation with select editors.

So how did this happen?

Our art director, Kendra. She called the book to my attention. She liked it, a lot, and not just because her husband is an old friend of yours.

A friend of mine? Who?

Jared James. A former student, I believe.

I gasped. *Jared?*

At a staff party recently, he told me you were the real deal. That's a quote. And I see that now.

Oh my, I murmured. *Please thank Kendra and ask her to tell Jared I think of him with great affection. You might say he was my muse.*

I believe the same can be said for you.

How so?

He's a lit professor. He said you inspired him.

My heart swelled. Something good had come from the lunch after all.

The novel is good, Sara. I appreciate your compassion. And your outrage. Nothing I like better than a woman who stands up, even a white woman.

I shook my head in resignation. *Nothing to lose.*

Must be nice, he said somberly, tenuous stature ever-present for even the most successful black man.

I wasn't sure what came over me, but I reached up and wrapped my arms around his back and he, caught off guard, hugged me in return. Seconds later we released and I turned on my heels to walk away, marching decisively with head held high. I was not sorry for anything I had written or said, even if for naught.

Weeks later, I watched a disturbing video on the evening news – a statuesque dark brown woman wearing an African-print halter dress and a head wrap, her shoulders shimmering in the light like freshly tilled earth, stood her ground starkly alone before a troop of riot police dressed in black body armor. With their faces obscured by helmets and clubs raised in their hands, they were as ominous and heinous as the Klu

Klux Klan dressed in white. A standoff it was, riveting and terrifying, and that footage was shared far and wide for days on television and on the Internet, and went viral on social media.

The woman stood in silent protest against yet another police shooting of a young black man and in that dramatic solo stance, she became a celebrity: a poster-girl for resistance. In a subsequent interview, she said she was not by nature an agitator, but she felt she had to show her solidarity.

Because, she said, *I love my people.*

I stared at her image over and over again, in awe. I admired her idealism, her integrity, and, oddly, I also envied her, despite the circumstance. I so wished, as I had when I was a child, and again, years later, with Jared, and many times since, I wished I too might feel pride in my people.

The Devoted Teacher

From the top of the hill, there is a grand sweeping view of the Pacific Ocean, and every morning, Frida searches for the craggy silhouette of Catalina Island on the horizon. Often, shrouded by a marine layer – despite southern California's reputation for sunshine, there are many hazy mornings – the land mass seems merely a low-lying cloud. Frequently invisible. Another of the great mysteries of the natural world Frida contemplates on her walk to work.

Her face is scrubbed to shining and shoulder-length hair still damp. She locks the front door to her cottage, the small craftsman-style structure nearly obscured by condominium complexes that have taken over the hillside, and heads to the corner where she stops to gaze at the expanse. The morning ritual.

The cottage where Frida resides is four blocks from the apartment complex where she lived with her father most of her life. When she graduated college, he suggested she might save on rent by living with him.

After all, he said. *What will I do with the spare room? I don't expect visitors.*

Frida kindly insisted a grown woman requires independence. What she never said was that she felt she had earned liberation after a lifetime as a surrogate wife.

She dutifully cooked for her father on Sundays – pots of stew or hearty soups, so he would have leftovers – and tended to him when he was ill. When he died, she scrubbed every inch of the apartment, painted the walls butter yellow and sold the place to a retired couple wanting to downsize. She put the proceeds away for a rainy day, although she's not sure what she would do with herself if she weren't teaching.

Today, the gray of the sky blends with the gray of the sea, as if no horizon at all. Is it no wonder, she ponders, that at one time many people believed, some still do, the earth is flat?

She begins her walk, maintaining a steady even pace, timed to arrive early and use this half-hour to review plans for the day. It is mid-fall, three months into the school year. The morning air is chilly, the sun rising slowly. Along the way, she inhales the familiar woodsy scent of chaparrals and seaside daisies, the musty fragrance of sage.

This morning Frida is less contemplative than usual. She's been unusually agitated and uneasy of late. Losing track of time. Relentlessly hungry, but nothing tastes right. At night, she slips quickly into a deep sleep, only to wake at dawn listless and slow to focus. A subtle ache at her brow suggests a change in the barometric pressure, the way she feels when hot dry Santa Ana winds blow in, although the weather forecast predicts no significant difference. Climate is stable in this part of the world, as a rule, but she would welcome a change, anything that might alter the feel of the air or the intensity of light in the sky, and take the edge off whatever it is that ails her.

Frida teaches at the public elementary school a half-mile away and unless the weather is inclement beyond the morning mist, she walks. For fifteen years she has taught third grade. This school year, however, she has been assigned to first grade. The new principal, the third in her tenure, a stout woman with a long shadow, dropped into her classroom at the end of June to pronounce the appointment. Frida was stripping bulletin boards and scrubbing shelves. She had already bagged chunks of chalk, pencil stubs, watercolors and brushes, and boxed spare construction and writing paper. A pile of readers on the floor waited shelving.

Frida stood when the principal walked in and when she removed one of the yellow rubber gloves she wore to shake hands, Mrs. Carter's hand felt as rubbery as the glove.

I've decided to assign you to first grade, she stated, nodding emphatically with a self-satisfied smile. *Variety is the spice of life, they say, and it's good for educators to shake up their routine, wouldn't you agree?* She didn't wait for a response. *The littles, that's what I call them, they need someone with your credentials and your reputation.*

Frida never imagined she had a reputation. She earned a teacher's license at the state university and five years later completed an online master's degree in early childhood education. She shows up, every day, absent only ten days all these years, when she simply could not move her body, and manages her class with every ounce of energy and compassion she has. Although she is cordial with fellow teachers, she never joins faculty committees and socializes only at obligatory events. She pays no mind to administrative matters beyond paperwork and regulations. At the end of each day, she trudges back up the hill to the mystery and mythology books she borrows weekly from the local library or the television series lined-up for viewing on her DVR.

For Frida, only the children matter.

It never occurred to her to argue the change in assignment and she felt deflated all summer, as if she'd failed in some way. Nevertheless, she devoted the break to brushing up on the current research on early reading and she studied the children's kindergarten reports, which remarked perfunctorily on how well versed they were, or not, with letters and numbers, and which had yet to recognize the key sight words or learned to follow a series of instructions. She ignored behavioral ratings; they are still so young. Impressionable. They need time to grow. Their intellect and their emotions are as fresh as newborn and their first grade experience as crucial to their futures as mother's milk.

Frida believes this is of particular importance for the students at this school: the children who live at the bottom of the hill and on the lower elevation of every measurable spectrum. The sooner she taps their curiosity and imagination the better and she has decided to be more than a guide – she will be their advocate. Something akin to a fairy godmother.

Children have always been drawn to Frida. May have something to do with large bright eyes and a body as skimpy and fluid as a rag doll. Perhaps her dark thick hair and porcelain skin, like a fairy tale heroine, and a smile tinged with anticipation, as if waiting for something promised long ago, like the pot of gold at the end of the rainbow or the kiss of a prince to break an evil spell. Children, she believes, see her as she is.

She stops a short way down the hill to watch rays of sun scatter across the houses below. Sidewalks on this path are wide and clean, bounded by stone walls heaving with pink and red Bougainvillea. Palm trees wave in the wind. She likes the way the light plays off the angularity of rooftops. As a child, walking this same route to this same school, she imagined she lived in a charmed forest.

Dog-walkers and power-walkers pass. *Good morning*, they chirp.

Another lovely day, Frida responds.

She never stops to chat and no one presses her to. They see the weighty book bag. The plain clothes and the earnest expression. Teachers may not receive adequate remuneration, but they are esteemed, Frida believes, if only for their willingness to spend day after day with a flock of lively children and by keeping them occupied, and safe, allow parents to do whatever they need to do, or whatever they would rather do with their days.

Frida's students are primarily the children of Mexican-Americans. They live in duplexes or triplexes or apartments bunched together on the densely populated streets off Pacific Coast Highway. Some are so-called dreamers, imported by immigrant parents, others born to the green-card holders and naturalized citizens who tend gardens, clean houses or service the hotels and restaurants dotting the beach cities along the southern coast like a strand of pearls.

In years past, children up the hill who attended this school were the progeny of pioneers from the east, hippies from the north or settlers from Los Angeles seeking a modern suburban outpost. Now, the more affluent children living on the coast or up the hill attend a new school inland or private schools elsewhere, leaving the in-town school to wither with the landscape that surrounds it.

Frida has watched for years as public schools serving poor populations steadily deteriorate. Facilities languish, supplies are limited and faculties oppressed by a steady onslaught of administrative assignments and curriculum revisions. She believes teachers are the bedrock of good schooling and they must focus on students – *eyes on the prize*, her father used to say – as blind as possible to policy that fluctuates on the wind. She thinks about this too on her daily walks, as a rule.

Cars rush down the hill as if on a speedway, their motors revved or, more frequently now, secreting the drone of hybrid and electric engines that make them sound like hovercrafts. Frida supposes, before long, they will be, and commuters might someday be transported long distances on high-speed rail, maybe even in suction tubes. Progress, she knows, is inevitable. She doesn't entirely tune out the world. She listens to radio news in the morning and watches TV news at dinner, although averting eyes and ears from invective rhetoric and the horrors of human existence.

She is particularly disturbed by the situation facing migrants at the Mexican border. Less than a two-hour drive from her home, children are being torn from their families, housed in cages or with strangers. Families living in squalor in the shadow of walls. Do those in charge realize there is no more traumatic experience for a child than to be separated from a parent? No matter the parent, no matter the reason. She sometimes believes she can hear their cries at night and she can only imagine how tormented local families must be over what's happening. She so much admires the volunteers who drive down to the border on weekends to bring food and supplies and a sliver of hope to the hopeless. She should go with them, but she cannot bring herself to go. She cannot bear the thought of their living conditions. She prays for them, every night, but otherwise directs her attention only to issues that may impact her own children.

Monday, Wednesday and Friday, at exactly the same time, she's greeted by William Thompson, Billy, he's called, on his morning constitutional. Billy is a compact man with thinning gray hair and a weathered complexion. He walks up and down the hill five times and then to a café for coffee and a cinnamon Danish.

Morning dear Freddy, he calls out with a grin, tipping his Dodgers baseball cap. He bestowed that nickname upon her when she was a little girl.

Morning, Mr. Bill, she answers.

They don't stop, she on her way to work and he on the exercise regimen he has been persuaded will guarantee longevity. He only recently gave up surfing and paddles a kayak instead to ride the waves. Always in flip-flops, he moves sluggishly, plagued by flat arches and swollen arthritic knees, none of which has altered his cheerfulness. He played gin rummy and watched football and baseball with Frida's father for forty years and in the years since her father and Billy's wife died, with a posse of fellow aged surf-dudes at a sports bar.

Her father was not one to surf. He feared the undertow. On occasion he dipped his toes into the foam, but he never encouraged Frida to frolic in the waves, preferring to slouch in a beach chair reading while she molded sandcastles. He kept good cheer and irascibility equally close to his vest, perking up only while watching sports, during which he shouted at the screen as if he were in the bleachers, his whole body swelling or deflating depending on the outcome. As a girl, Frida sat at the edge of the couch while her father and Billy rooted for their teams, cheering or booing with them. In adolescence, she sat at the kitchen table doing homework, amused by their hoots and hollers. These days, she listens to the commentators on the Sunday sports channel and when they raise their voices, she watches the replay, which she imagines would make her father happy.

She prefers school days. She awakens with the sun and moves through the day in a comparable arc. On shorter days, like these, she makes sure to be at the top of the hill when the sun falls into the sea, then shuts herself in for the night, as if she might vanish in the dark.

Saturdays, Frida tutors English as a second language at the community center and afterward joins fellow instructors for food and drink – margarita is her preference. Some Saturdays last all day at one or another bar or pool hall and, now and then, she spends the night with one of the mechanics, pool cleaners, landscapers or medical technicians, also Lyft or Uber drivers, who grew up here. Most were her classmates at the school at the bottom of the hill and through high school. She knows them. She can trust them to be kind. No obligations and no illusions, merely companions of the night who evaporate like the mist in the light of day.

There was someone once she thought might be her own. A boy, not yet a man, who moved on, in the search, he claimed, for a more stimulating life. She occasionally scans his Facebook page, where he posts photographs with his wife and sons hiking at state parks or rowing between islands in the Pacific Northwest. A stimulating enough life, she imagines.

A classroom filled with kinetic children is sufficient stimulation for Frida, although, at fifteen, she toyed with the idea of becoming a flight attendant; she envied the uniforms and was intrigued with the idea of travel as a career rather than an indulgence. In college, after watching an actress better known for sex appeal portray a lawyer, she was briefly stirred with the nobility of defending and protecting civil rights, but she knew she lacked the grit.

In truth, there was never a doubt Frida would become a teacher, like her father, a life-long middle school science teacher, and her mother, a professor of European art history, before she married. Imprinted as well by all the teachers who modeled the role at the front of classrooms throughout her childhood, cologne following in their footsteps like a trail of crumbs to safety for the motherless girl.

Just before the very bottom of the hill, Frida turns south to walk three blocks to the school. This is where the landscape turns mangy, and yet, defying the odds, succulents sprout flowers between strangling weeds. She too feels like a bud reaching for the light, particularly since an encounter with the principal last week, which began in the faculty lunchroom.

Eight teachers surrounded the communal table, the others on playground or cafeteria duty. All Caucasian, middle class, career educators, the youngest naïve and fervent, the elders with shoulders slumped and bodies going to flab. They munched on cold cut sandwiches or salad greens from plastic containers. They drank from stainless steel water bottles or paper coffee cups.

I wonder if what we do is enough? Frida remarked. She hadn't meant to speak aloud. Small talk is the custom among teachers on break. However, once the words spilled out, she felt obligated to elaborate. *What I mean is, how do we help our children move beyond the core?*

The newest faculty member spoke up. A slim girl with sun-bleached blonde hair and a deep tan, she teaches kindergarten. She leaned forward to share what she learned in graduate school, as if the veterans might have forgotten.

Whatever the disparity in their maturity or intellect, or background, focus on the fundamentals is essential. And, you know, this is the time to identify the learning challenges that will hold them back, especially the kids who did not attend nursery school. That's the imperative, right?

She posed her response to the table, but faced Frida, who nodded without a word because she loathes formulaic responses and, although she started this conversation, she had no intention of proceeding.

The principal walked in at that moment and asked to meet with the sixth grade teacher. She smiled at the group, a wan smile without baring teeth. Gray hairs sprouted at her temples, although she is not much older than Frida. She was dressed in one of a handful of slim-fitting wrap dresses she wears most of the time, in shades of gray or black or brown that accentuate a complexion more faded than fair. Most teachers, all but two are female, wear slacks with billowy blouses or T-shirts so they might easily slither under desks to retrieve pencils or crouch on the floor with the children. A principal wouldn't have to do that.

All good here? Mrs. Carter asked, a question they understood to be rhetorical, although the novice responded.

We were talking, well, Frida posed the question if we do enough to compensate for the limitations of our students.

Frida bristled. She might have said that was not at all the question she had asked, but she refrained.

The principal nodded thoughtfully and said, *All youngsters are tabula rasa. I don't care what their circumstance is. Yes, there is genetics and home life, but they rise to the standards set for them. Students are here to learn and we are here to prepare them to move on to the next grade. That's what we do.*

The teachers around the table sat up in their chairs, anxious to hear how the typically taciturn Frida might respond, so she felt compelled to speak.

When you've spent more time with these children and these families, you will see how much they want to learn and most come primed to learn. What they need is encouragement. They need confidence in their capacity to learn. We can help them feel they are citizens of a larger world.

Mrs. Carter nodded again, as if Frida's words meant something to her, and then glanced at her watch and said, *I have something pressing, but do stop by my office, any time, to discuss. My door is always open.*

What would be the point of an open door without an open mind? Frida wondered. She has observed narrow minds in too many adults over the years – her father and friends, neighbors, shopkeepers, and yes, teachers – all those whom she has come to categorize as givers or takers, thinkers or talkers, truth-tellers or mythmakers. The adults resistant, at best, or condescending, at worst, to those they think of as lesser.

Children are no lesser for being smaller, and no lesser for having less. A child, to Frida's mind, is not so much a tabula rasa as a jewel to be mined. Schooling is the excavation, not the polish.

Every morning, when Frida arrives at school, she shakes her head twice – left to right, right to left – to clear her mind. She clocks in and heads to the teacher's lounge where she tucks the insulated bag containing her tuna salad or cheese sandwich into the refrigerator. She unlocks the door to her classroom, hangs her jacket across the back of her chair and piles her attendance record and lesson plans on the desk. She opens a window to welcome the morning air and takes one deep breath in, another out, to lock in good intentions. She stands at the classroom door like a palace guard and greets each child with a welcome smile and a pat on the back. She used to give them a hug, but that is frowned upon now, as if all teachers, like priests, might be predatory. One of these days, she imagines, they will all have to pass through metal detectors and she might be asked to carry a gun, which she will never do, although she would protect her children with her life.

Welcome to class today, she says to students as they arrive, by name. Many common names, like Juan, Pedro, José, Jesus, Maria, Fernanda, Alexandra. Some more distinctive, like Ursula and Lucinda, Arturo and Eduardo, or literary, like Sylvia or Boris. The first week of school, she gave them bins filled with art supplies and while they created a child's version of abstract art, she invited one by one to her desk to get to know them.

She learned that Manuel, an agile boy whose skinny legs seem in perpetual motion, joins his father after school to wash windows, skittering to rooftops to clear cobwebs under the eaves. Juanita, soft-spoken and hesitant, accompanies her mother to clean houses. She said she likes to sweep the floors, because the whoosh of a broom reminds her of the wind. Mauricio's father is a house painter and he proudly stirs the paint with a stick to maintain its consistency. Multi-colored smudges stain his tiny fingernails like polish. Lucinda, tall for her age, pulls thick hair back with a headband, but tendrils spill tenderly around her plump face. She stocks inventory after school at her uncle's market in town, where neighbors find supplies of jalapeño peppers and nopales, cotija cheese and 5-pound bags of rice.

All help at home with the babies of their families, or they are the babies, and all have an ineffable sense of belonging, even the shy ones who answered without meeting her eyes, at first, and before long snuggle close in the sharing circle as if her own.

Day after day, Frida drills her children in phonetics and vocabulary, the sequence of days and seasons and holidays, and arithmetic. They play with clay, they paint at easels, they paste magazine clippings to construction papers. She reads to them from an expanded library she has chosen to enrich their comprehension, stories that will help them evolve into human beings capable of empathy and fortitude, what they will most need to climb the hills ahead.

When she explained her philosophy to the parents on open school night a few weeks into the term, most nodded in agreement without comment; others expressed their approval with grateful smiles. She wasn't sure they all understood what she was saying and she would have preferred to deliver part of her presentation in Spanish – she learned in middle school and kept it up – but faculty is required to speak English at all times. Frida knows that whatever they understood from her talk or from the weekly postings to parents, all they want for their children is to learn what they must learn to make a decent living. Frida, who grew up at the top of the hill, wants far more for them, and she is increasingly determined to pave their way.

Today, at the end of the day, instead of going straight home, Frida walks a few blocks south to watch preschoolers on the playground at a Montessori school. These children are light-skinned. They dress in stylish clothes that fit perfectly and bear no sign of having been washed hundreds of times and faded on a line in the sun. They run around in sparkling sneakers with recognizable logos. Their games are inventive and conversations filled with unbridled precocity. This school encourages students to consider every lesson embedded in play and playthings and to thoughtfully weigh their options. Every time she watches them, her spirits are buoyed by their ebullience, although simultaneously dispirited by the inequity between her children and these.

One of her earliest memories is an argument between her parents having to do with Montessori school. She was not yet three years old and her mother must have been lobbying for the alternative school, while her father, the traditionalist, obdurate. The word Montessori itself, so foreign and complex, made Frida fear her mother might whisk her away to England, where the grandparents she knew only through postcards and pictures lived. At the same time, she was excited by the prospect, picturing London as a vast metropolis of imperial buildings flanking broad boulevards, blanketed in autumn with the red and gold leaves of ancient trees and in winter with snow. She imagined rainy days and foggy nights and in later years, after she read *Wuthering Heights*, she felt drawn to the moors. Her mother once described her homeland as an island in the mist and this comes to mind whenever the marine layer settles over the horizon.

Soon after that argument, Frida's mother left home. She whispered something to little Frida who was half-asleep that early morning and could not decipher her mother's words. She never got the chance to ask.

Eight weeks later, her father moved them from their little house to the apartment complex where Billy's wife would watch out for her when her father was working. She attended a church nursery school where she learned to identify shapes and colors and sit quietly during reading hour, but it was in kindergarten, at the little school at the bottom of the hill, where the holiness of the classroom took root. Words adorned bulletin boards. Books filled the shelves. Shafts of light streamed into the room all day. She was never alone. Weekends, holidays and summers, she counted days until back in class, which her father interpreted as a superior intellect, rather than the despondency of a discarded child.

She received birthday and Christmas greetings, postcards and trinkets. Her mother called every Sunday, then, over time, alternating Sundays, and then, only on special occasions. Billy's wife explained that her mother took a teaching post in Lyon, France, and remarried. Nothing more was said and Frida never asked, because to ask, she knew, might result in greater knowing than she could endure. When she graduated college, she received $200 and an airline ticket to Paris, which she never acknowledged.

Her mother in effect disappeared like dandelion petals in the wind, leaving behind only the Mexican name she bestowed on her daughter as an homage to her favorite artist, and which makes Frida feel a special kinship to her students.

Despite misgivings, Frida made an appointment to meet with Mrs. Carter. The office manager greeted her with the expression of exasperation with which she has greeted Frida for years. She pointed to a chair to indicate there was a wait and turned her attention back to a mound of paperwork. When Frida was invited in, Mrs. Carter gestured to take a seat opposite where she stood at an elevated desktop typing.

Okay, done, Mrs. Carter said, with an emphatic final keyboard click.

Frida said, *I would like to take the children on a field trip, but I was informed this is not permitted in first grade. I wasn't aware of that policy.*

That's new. System-wide. Not until third grade. They're so young, the liability, you know. Time enough for that.

Never too soon to explore the world.

What's so important they cannot get in the classroom or on the grounds?

For a start, more time outdoors, not just on the playground. Imagine if they were encouraged to lie on the grass and observe cloud formations. Take a hike or cultivate an herb garden...

I'm in favor of gardens, we should look into that here, said Mrs. Carter in earnest, *but budgets are tight and we have just six hours a day to teach them all they need to learn. I'm afraid cloud formations will not improve reading scores. Where would you want to take them anyway?*

To the nursery. A four-block walk. No bus.

The nursery? To look at plants?

Frida smiled. *Color. Texture. Dimension and shape. Scent and touch. Their first lesson in photosynthesis. A wonderful place to enhance a child's awareness of the planet.*

Mrs. Carter stared at Frida, frankly confused, then picked up and waved a bound document in one hand. *Listen Frida, this report confirms that if children are not reading at grade level by third grade, they are four times more likely to drop out of high school. The children here need an incentive to stay, not having, shall we say, the more accomplished role models. Let's just stay on task, shall we?*

Frida walked home slowly that day. A stinging heat burrowed under her skin and a heaviness in her chest, as if a great burden rested there. She felt she would rather be somewhere or someone else, a feeling she rarely has. Nevertheless, she stopped to enjoy sea breezes blowing through her hair. She watched lizards scurry across her path, as if guiding her home. She picked up the pace to race the sun to its finish line. At the top of the hill, she turned to watch swaths of gold and orange rising from the horizon line, sprayed with slivers of pink as if paint had been flung from the sea.

Sunsets late in the year and in winter along the western coast are especially vibrant. This has to do, her father once explained, with light passing through more of the atmosphere before visible to the naked eye.

The blue light scatters, he told the young Frida, *illuminating reds and oranges. Compensation for the chill, I suppose. For shorter days and long nights.*

Staring at that vista, rife with possibilities, Frida knew what she must do. Along the next morning walk, and again on the walk home, she devised a plan. She will take a stand for her children. She will scatter the light. She has only to wait for the right moment.

Frida is expert at waiting. She waited week after week for her mother's call. She waited a lifetime for her father to reach out for a fuller life. She waited for another boy to take her into his heart. No matter the waiting was never rewarded. Waiting. Patience. Adaptation. She believes these qualities are essential and in shorter supply these days, more so with every dispassionate politician and misguided administrator.

On the walk the next morning, she ponders what roads will be like when driverless cars are commonplace. Teenagers may no longer have to learn to drive, just as they no longer use a dictionary or an encyclopedia. She remembers fondly when her father taught her to drive, no matter how nervous she was and how stern he could be.

Always take a 360-degree view, he instructed, cautioning her to watch for pedestrians in an automobile-centric society. *Patience, Frida,* he advised, as she waited to make a turn or ease onto the freeway. *Patience, my girl, is everything.*

She wishes now she had asked what her father waited for and what was his reward.

Frida waited three months – beyond winter holiday, Martin Luther King Day and Presidents' Day. She slept poorly, she ate poorly, she obsessed over the obstacles her children face every day. She prayed every night for the children at the border. An opportunity at last arrived when the principal announced she would attend a state conference the following week and the marginally effectual vice-principal would take her place. The next day, Frida sent notes home to the parents announcing a field trip the following Thursday. She printed the trip title in green marker: THE GREEN DAY. She told parents the children would walk four blocks to the nursery to study local plant life. Lunch would be provided – no expense, no bus, and no permission slip required. She told them there will be a later pick-up that day, to make the trip as full an experience as possible, and provided her cell phone number for questions. No one made contact because the parents don't know or have forgotten that a permission slip is always required. They trust Frida. They trust she will nurture and protect their children, which she will, in this case from a bureaucracy that no longer has their best interests at heart.

During the three days before the trip, Frida devotes afternoon lessons to the color green, which she ties to the imminent arrival of spring. She displays a color wheel with images of the many different shades of green and recites their proper names, which the children echo triumphantly, rolling the words in their mouths like candy: lime, shamrock, fern, pine, forest, seafoam. She encourages them to list everyday green things: traffic lights, palm trees, avocados. She presents photographs of tourmaline and emerald jewelry, drawings of birds with bright green crowns, and paintings like Monet's *Woman in Green*, Van Gogh's *Green Wheat*, and Rothko's *Green Red on Orange*, which they stare at longer than the others, mesmerized by its deceptive simplicity.

Late Thursday morning, after the last green lesson, after playground time and after lunch and bathroom break, she marches them out a side entrance and off school grounds. No one notices them leave or, if they do, no one stops them. Once out of sight of the school, she lines the children up to place four-leaf clover stickers on their shirts to mark their group and mark the day.

The children are exceptionally animated and she cautions them, as their parents surely have, to be on their best behavior.

Speak in your inside voices, she says. *Hold hands with your buddy when you walk and raise your hand if you need my attention.*

She trusts they will follow directions and in turn she will give them a wide birth.

She leads them to the hill and down to the nursery. The manager, one of her weekend comrades, greets them like dignitaries and escorts them from the section crowded with spring flowers to the succulents, and to an area packed with dwarf trees and tall grasses. He explains how plants use water and air to grow and how they exhale what humans need to breathe. He points out oddly shaped cactus and miniature palms.

He explains which are indigenous and they echo the word like a magic spell. They peer closely, they stick their noses close to sniff, like puppies, and their little fingers trace the silhouettes of leaves, delighting in their velvety softness or sharp edges.

After sufficient time for juvenile attention spans, and after they show appreciation to the manager with applause, Frida lines them up in handholding pairs to begin the climb up the hill. She leads them in singing a song she discovered online: *Green as the grass, green as a bean, green is the color of summer leaves...*

They chant in unison, her voice guiding them as she trots backwards at the front of the line. They sing and shout and giggle as they march, and they don't notice they have passed the turn to school. They follow Frida along the bright wide sidewalks and past the pink Bougainvillea. Although their little legs grow tired, enthusiasm sustains them, and when at last they arrive at the top of the hill, Frida shepherds them through the gate to her cottage.

There are twenty-two students in attendance; three are home with colds. The little house contains one large room for living, cooking and dining, with a bedroom and bathroom to the side. Dark wood floors contrast with whitewashed walls. Triangular windows flank a vaulted ceiling, ushering in sunlight by day and starlight at night.

Frida has moved her furniture to the edges to blanket the floor with quilts and she sits the children there, assigning two to distribute the sugar cookies she baked at dawn and decorated with green icing. She places them one by one from the cooling rack on to green napkins. She hands out individual milk cartons and then squeezes in with them on the floor, encouraging the children to discuss the plants they liked best, and why, and catalog again the many shades of green.

They chatter as they munch cookies and lick the icing off their fingertips. They slurp milk through tiny built-in straws to the gurgling last drops. Laughter fills the cottage to the rafters and Frida feels the presence of longing to which she never yields. She chose a life devoted to other people's children and today, today her children are home at last.

Daylight outside her windows steadily dims. She has turned off her phone so she will not hear the calls of parents who, at this late hour, must be anxious for their children's return. The assistant principal must be pacing the sidewalk. Mrs. Carter might have been called. Police will soon arrive at school, red-spinning lights declaring a crisis.

Why don't they realize there is no crisis? Her students are where they should be, with their beloved teacher. At the top of the hill. She should not have to surrender them to less than they deserve.

The children tire. They lean against each other. Lupita whines for her mother. Manuel tussles with Oscar. Sylvia rests her head in her lap. Pedro stares at Frida with suspicion.

Patience, children, she urges, as she waits for dusk, hoping for the crowning glory of this day.

At the right moment, she stands and marshals the children outside to watch the sun's final descent behind Catalina Island. The golden ball illuminates the landmass from behind, sinking steadily to the sea, revealing the island's cliffs and angular peaks. She was so hoping for a green flash, an atmospheric play of light believed to reveal at sunset, but rarely observed. Frida and her father often watched for the mythical green ray for the second or two it is said to crest along the upper rim of the sun. She has yet to witness the phenomenon. Still, she waits. Day after day, year after year, she waits.

Juanita shuffles closer to Frida. *Maestra, I want to go home*, she whimpers.

Pedro stands and says, in the voice of a natural leader, *we should go now, Miss Frida.*

Come closer, Niños, Frida coos as she waves her arms wide to gather them. They move as one into a crescent around her. *Close your eyes, go ahead, just for a moment*, she says, as she detects the sound of sirens at the bottom of the hill.

Most of the children close their eyes. Her heart swells with their innocence. She speaks slowly, melodiously, as if reading aloud a fairy tale.

I'm going to tell you something wondrous. Keep your eyes closed, that's right, as if you are dreaming. Now, imagine a huge green glow in the night sky. Like a giant green cloud. A green brighter and more spectacular than any green. This is called the Aurora Borealis, which happens off the island of Iceland, near Greenland, a place far far away, but closer than the stars. Someday, you will go there to see this beautiful feat of nature. You will see many great marvels in your life, but this may be the greatest of all. That sky will be luminous, that means shining or shimmering, like the light of a full moon, like lightning, like fireworks, and more amazing than any sky anyone has ever seen on this great earth.

Such a thing makes you believe everything is possible. I want you to remember this, my children. Anything is possible. And this is just one of many great things you will see as you grow. You will. Yes, you will. Never settle for less.

Trust in Miss Frida, Niños. All things come to those who wait.

The Divorcée

Her ex-husband would be late. This Sharon knew for sure. The only time he had been prompt was their first date. He was waiting for her then. Never again, delayed even on their wedding day, albeit a matter of moments, and ever since, his inner clock off roughly fifteen minutes. Noticeable, yet, inexplicably, offensive to no one but Sharon.

Knowing this about him, as a longtime wife knows the intimate habits and eccentricities of a man, she dressed slowly and drove slowly the short distance to downtown from her little house in Providence, Rhode Island, far enough off the beaten track to escape swarms of students and tourists, close enough to the university to minimize her commute. She deliberately, almost in pantomime, sauntered from the parking spot she found a block away to the French restaurant she had recommended for dinner, and then stopped at the entrance to glance at her watch. Just three minutes late. She had to laugh at herself. Sharon is never tardy, even on purpose.

Red was already there. The moment she walked in she caught a glimpse of him at the bar, unmistakable even with his back turned to her. Half-seated on a bar stool, he leaned on one long leg, the other bent beneath him with his foot on the cross piece like a cowboy at a saloon. Instead of a shot of whiskey, however, he held a glass of red wine, an open bottle nearby on the bar. As unexpected as timeliness.

He turned toward the entrance, watching for her more than sensing her, as if she might have missed him, and when he saw her, he stood, always the gentleman, trained from birth to stand in the presence of elders or strangers and women of all ages. She paused to take in all six feet four inches of him. The broad squared shoulders shielding a disproportionately narrow neck. Exceedingly long arms. Legs like tree trunks. Like the stick figures her sons used to draw of the family, the three of them diminishing in size order from Red's elongated torso. After their first date, she described him to a friend as a lean friendly bear with strawberry blonde hair, and in those days, to be in his embrace was as reassuring as thrilling. Now, nearing seventy, he remains fit, although no longer the athlete he was in his youth, neither the strapping engineer she met on that first date at a pub in Boston.

Forty years since they were introduced. Forty years since the short courtship, during which she tallied similarities and ignored differences.

People do not have to match, she told her doubting roommate. *They have only to blend*, she insisted, in the spirit of infatuation.

How naïve, she was, in retrospect. And now, here they are, on another first date of sorts. He retired, and she, at sixty-five, in the life she intended.

Red reached for her hands, clasping them between his as if old friends, much like the overly familiar men she meets on occasion at restaurant bars on an arranged date she always regrets. They hugged, with genuine affection, not tentatively like so many divorced couples do. No pretense between them, not now. Within her grasp, he felt bonier than he seemed from afar. Muscles softening with age, she assumed. He may have finally cut back on his evening snack of a tall glass of chocolate milk, a childhood indulgence that stuck. The night he proposed, he asked if she would promise to keep chocolate milk, whole milk specifically, and crunchy cookies, always on hand. She kept that promise, despite her resistance. She kept most of her promises, except the one that mattered most: *until death do us part.*

She didn't comment on his frame, to avoid any semblance of sarcasm and because she had no wish to yield to a maddening inequity of age – he trimmer, she plumper.

He proffered the bottle of wine and she noticed an empty glass already on the bar. *Or do you still prefer white,* he asked, as he grabbed his jacket off an adjacent bar stool and pulled it out for her.

White, dry, she requested of the bartender.

I have a fine Sancerre, he answered, and she nodded enthusiastically.

Still ABC, I see. Anything but chardonnay, he translated for the bartender, who smiled without comment as he pulled a bottle from the cooler.

Sharon settled on the stool, spread her coat across her lap and reached under the bar top, searching for a hook to hang her purse.

One of those small engineering feats that makes sense, Red said, as if she were a woman at a bar he didn't know but would like to know.

And you've switched to wine? she asked. *No more the brown spirits man?*

All their years together he drank bourbon, sometimes scotch, like his father, always neat and always premium labels. He shrugged. *Even this old dog learns a few new tricks.*

Sharon was struck by the unusual humility, but she dismissed her inner skeptic in favor of cordiality.

Nice place, by the way, Red said.

I'd hoped we'd be early enough to beat the crowd, but maybe not.

Bustling, I believe, is the term.

Too much?

Not at all, my hearing is holding up.

The modern urban bistro. Sound ricochets from wall to wall.

An architect I worked with says the décor is meant to impel liveliness. Promotes turnover too, I suppose.

But do they factor in lost customers?

Folds into the algorithm.

They both chuckled. Sharon, however, felt badly; she should have suggested a quieter place.

I like the vibe, and I like the open flow, he said, as if reading her mind, something he never mastered in marriage, nor ever tried to master, she contended.

Yes, there is that, she agreed. *I think they call it new-wave industrial.*

Or, paradoxically, retro-modern.

Paradoxical indeed, Sharon said.

Sharon once preferred more traditional space, furnishings too, and in this, they were the same. They resided for nearly thirty years in a Victorian home they refurbished over time, and then took nearly as long to furnish, filling living spaces with plush seating, heavy drapes and middle-eastern rugs in subtle colors. These days, she gravitates to minimalism, even in a classically colonial city like this. Like this restaurant, the site of a former textile factory. Or was it a silversmith? She's forgotten. Brick walls flanked the length. Tall ceilings exposed aluminum air ducts. Floors made of reclaimed planks of wood. Mismatched chairs surrounded tables topped with marble or tin. The square bar anchored the space under a myriad of pin lights, conjuring a nighttime sky.

Not exactly cozy, or French for that matter, rather expansive, she said, opening her arms wide, as if presenting the bistro.

A word she might use to describe herself in later life, Sharon thought with satisfaction. Expansive.

The bartender delivered her wine and as she took a sip she noticed a disappointed expression on Red's face. He would have preferred to toast, always wanting to punctuate a moment, but at that moment, Sharon needed the wine to still her nerves. She could not imagine why. She knows this man inside out and after all these years, nothing he might say or do will surprise her. They long ago successfully navigated their parting. Healed and hearty, she often says. Nonetheless, she's been jittery all day.

When did you get in? she asked.

Late morning. Spent the afternoon wandering, shadowed by ghosts of colonists and revolutionaries. I drove over to Bristol too. Different from when I came down from graduate school a thousand years ago, although I cannot tell you what's changed and what hasn't. Little stays fixed in time, right?

Staying in town?

At the Omni. By the riverfront, that's definitely different. I strolled over to Brown, more impressive than I remember, although, as you once described, understated. I sort of hoped to run into you.

Sharon chuckled, even as she had the uneasy feeling her ex-husband was stalking her. She has so much enjoyed carving out her own turf in a place where he has no footprints.

I had office hours most of the afternoon. Good flight? she asked, shaking off the disquiet as the bartender set down an earthenware bowl filled with a mix of olives. Red grabbed a few and popped one into his mouth, cradling the others in his hand as if he might juggle.

Fine. Interesting, he mumbled as he spit a pit into his other hand to drop into the smaller empty bowl served with the larger, and in one smooth motion popped a second olive into his mouth. Synchronized, in effect, as if his hands and mouth were levered, which is the way Sharon came to picture him – mechanical, like a precision instrument. Like the AI and robotics he worked on the last decade of his career and still tinkered with in the tiny workshop he carved out of a closet in the back of his townhouse, so her sons have reported.

What was so interesting?

An older woman on the plane, much older, elderly one would say, kept asking me the same question, over and over again. Her daughter, definite resemblance, sat at the window, mother in the middle, me on the aisle, of course, and the daughter apologized. She thought I was bothered, which I wasn't. I insisted I didn't mind, but she made the mom switch seats anyway.

In the early days of their marriage, wherever they flew, Red claimed the aisle, needing to spread out those long legs, and Sharon, by default, sat in the cramped middle seat. After a time, she took to booking the opposite aisle seat. When they traveled as a family, each of their sons sat with a parent, the middle seat comfortable for children until they too sprouted tall and leggy and whined about being stuck in the middle, so she booked them into window seats. Everyone in position, Red used to say, and Sharon remembers thinking people should not line up like the connections on a circuit board.

I read a piece, a while back, Sharon mused, *about an older woman at a beauty salon. I think the New York Times magazine, that medical inquiry section?*

Do you still read the Times? The Tribune?

I prefer the Washington Post these days.

Not the ProJo?

She laughed. *Well, yes, that too. How did you know what our newspaper is called?*

I picked one up. Oldest continuously published paper in the country.

So they like to say.

Noteworthy, in this day and age.

True.

So, as I was saying, this woman in the article, every time she bent her head back to have her hair washed, she would sit back up and ask what time it was, then bend her head back, then sit up again and ask again. The young man washing her hair thought at first it was just odd, but then, when she seemed disoriented, they called paramedics. Turns out, every time she bent her head back, she moved into just the right position to compress the blood flow to her short-term memory. She never remembered asking the question or the answer. Not so much age, or dementia, but anatomy.

And I bet you think of that every time you have your hair done, Red said.

To punctuate the comment, he pressed a palm over his dome – an old habit of tidying hair no longer there. He was mostly bald by his forties and for years shaved resistant strands into a smooth shell. None left now, and at the top, which few see, a series of dents and scars, like craters on the surface of the moon, from one too many run-ins with low ceilings. The frequent subject of good-natured kidding by their sons.

In truth, Sharon was uncomfortable with her neck pressed against a hard metal sink at the salon and had taken to washing her hair herself beforehand, but she would not admit to that.

By the way, I like your hairdo, Red commented.

She had recently cropped her silvery hair and added ash brown lowlights, which she had sworn she'd never do, but she wasn't ready to go all the way to gray.

Thanks. Small concession to age, she said.

An air of distinction. Most flattering.

Gray works better for men.

I'll never know.

She smiled. *And you look well, very well. A slightly age-worn version of your younger self.*

You think?

He smiled, she returned the smile and took a sip of wine. She settled into the familiarity of him: his scent, always the same after-shave, subtle and woodsy. He still wore the dark-rimmed glasses he has worn for forty years, bifocal now, which partially veil unusually pale blue eyes, and the same type of clothes he's always worn, what they now call corporate casual: a crisp blue pinstripe shirt, open at the collar, tucked neatly into pressed trousers. He claimed from the first that it was difficult to think in a tie. On very special occasions, coerced into wearing a good suit or tuxedo, he was appeased only when Sharon insisted he looked like Warren Beatty at the Oscars.

The last time they were together, over a year ago, he wore a new suit for their younger son Brady's graduate school commencement in New York City. That was nearly two years to the day after older son Jamie graduated with his master's degree, in Philadelphia. Both boys worked or traveled for a time, before setting sights on graduate school, and at their recent celebration, surrounded by family members and a few close friends, Red pronounced, as if a personal achievement, that his sons were at last launched.

Sharon had a good laugh at his naiveté. *For the moment,* she observed, *although this generation shifts like the seasons. On the path to the paths not taken.*

Not like Red, who set his path to engineering in high school and never wavered, or Sharon, for that matter, who aspired to teach at the university level, like her father, who died a year after he retired from his post at Harvard, as if no further point to living. Red got his start in Boston and then founded a firm with his name, and two others, on the door, back in Chicago, his hometown.

At first, Sharon gave up her studies in favor of a paycheck while Red completed an apprenticeship and earned a reputation. By the time they settled and their income was more reliable, she was so long beyond her coursework, she would have had to start over, so she held at the master's level and took a position teaching literature at a local high school.

An academic has to go where the job is, she told friends. *A crapshoot to get the degree and then find no school in Chicago wants my specialty. Besides, I like having an income,* she insisted, determined to defend the adaptation to the needs of husband and sons.

She came to resent her limitations. In hindsight, she realized she should never have given up her own aspirations. Her choice, she acknowledged, although under some duress, she has often said. However she never gave up the ambition and five years ago, post-divorce, she moved east to complete her PhD in Victorian literature, with a concentration on Elizabeth Gaskell, novelist and social historian, and with a special fondness for the poets.

A poet and an engineer, she thought while she was dressing for her date earlier. She changed five times, she's not sure why. *Anyone could have seen we were not a good match,* she said aloud, a habit of late, living alone. *Anyone but me, that is.*

Been ages since we had dinner together, Red said, and she snapped back to attention.

Indeed, she answered, biting into an olive to still the rumbling in her stomach. *I was surprised when you said you were coming on business. What business?*

This and that, he answered, without elaboration.

Sharon, having listened for years to his rants over exasperating clients and projects run aground by risk-averse bureaucrats, had stopped caring, and she assumed he was happy to leave all that behind when he announced his retirement three years ago. Now, he has said, when mid-western winter settles in, he abandons the golf course and tennis court and curls up in his reading chair to catch up with piles of histories and biographies, and he binge-watches BBC mysteries or the plethora of thrillers and police procedurals she cannot abide. She imagines he delights in the freedom to enjoy without critique; she was never good at hiding her disdain for violence masquerading as theatre. She too has been freed to enjoy documentaries about a renowned chef, a filmmaker or feminist, or indulge a penchant for light comedies with sexy leading men.

She was about to inquire about members of his family when a hostess arrived to escort them to their table. Red left a tip on the bar and they followed her, half-filled wine glasses and nearly full bottle balanced precariously on a tray she held slightly aloft, to a table nestled into a quieter corner.

Good spot for conversation, Red said, as he held out her chair.

Although Sharon felt some redemption for the noise, the setting was painfully reminiscent of their last dinner together while married. Six years ago, almost to the day, also a busy bistro, where soon after they arrived, after a few sips of drinks and a few bits of small talk, Sharon announced they had come to the end.

The end of what? Red asked, as he bit into the bruschetta she had preordered.

The end of our marriage, Sharon answered.

Red looked at her with a confused expression, as if she had merely commented on a factoid from the newspaper. As her words settled in, he stared at her in stunned silence, as if they had not been heading this direction for years, as if she had never asked him to go to counseling, which he refused, and as if they were not the rusty bucket Sharon believed they were, leaking steadily until not one drop left. She held his gaze, expecting him to counter, cajole, detonate his anger, anything more than nothingness, but all he said was, *so it goes,* before he stood, looming over her briefly as she sat stony still, determined to stay in one piece, and then he gulped down the last of his bourbon and walked out of the restaurant. She was shaken by the finality. So long coming, the end seemed nonetheless inexplicable. Some time later, Red advised his sons that it's best not to flame a fire, a mantra for disengagement in matters too close to the bone.

What burns will eventually burn out, he said.

Yes, but who might be scorched in that fire?
Sharon countered. *Trust me,* she told the boys. *Where there's smoke, there will be fire, and nothing recovers from the ash.*

In my next life, I'd like to be a neurobiologist, study the brain, Red said, calling her back to attention.

I wonder if it's as complicated as it seems. Maybe the wiring just wears down, short-circuits, like an old lamp.

I'd find a way to diddle with the circuits.

A memory engineer, she quipped.

Red laughed, a loud anxious laugh, brasher than the remark warranted. A nervous habit she's seen countless times. Why would he be nervous? Perhaps the same reason she's been on edge all day. Now she wonders, what she should have considered sooner, he might be here to tell her something she will not want to hear. Something must be wrong.

Memory is selective, Red went on. *For example, at this moment, this discussion, the sounds and smells, the clothes we're wearing, like the blue of your dress, what would you call that, federal blue?*

She nodded.

Matches your eyes, by the way. So this is all being recorded in our memory centers, right? We'll recall the details tomorrow, the next day or next, but with diminishing accuracy. The specifics fuzzier. More to the point, we won't remember them the same way.

So true, Sharon said.

What I'll remember first and foremost of this evening is how lovely you look. Truly. Your new home, your pursuits, all serving you well, my dear.

He held up and tipped his wine glass to her and she responded the same. They clinked.

Here's to memory, he said, taking a swallow before he continued. *Although I do wonder if losing a bit of memory isn't a blessing. I mean, if you miss some of the details, a few contiguous distractions, there's a better appreciation of the day. Not burdened with what chore you haven't done or what project has yet to be completed. Or what book is waiting to be read. Of course, I would hate not recognizing people or not knowing where I belong, but not to sweat the small stuff, that suits me fine right now.*

Is that what retirement life is like? Letting go of the small stuff? Practicing mindfulness in your old age?

Ha! I'll leave that to Buddhists and Millennials. I'm just trying to loosen the reigns a bit, although, we both know, once an engineer, always an engineer. For us, it's all about the small stuff.

The small stuff, she thought, but not the conspicuously significant, like a wife taken for granted, a distant second to work and children, television sports and long hours in the garage workshop.

Maybe the woman on the plane who kept asking the same question had a need to know. Forgetting is not the same as not knowing, Sharon commented.

You've always had a way of getting to the heart of the thing, Red said, with a warm smile. *Must be all that poetry. 'Beauty is truth, truth beauty'... forgot the rest.*

The engineer quoting Keats? Flummoxed by the citation, and the praise, and increasingly uneasy about why he was here, her stomach rumbled with hunger and she picked up the menu. *Shall we order?*

You have a preference here?

The fish is always fresh. Salads yummy. And to match the retro-modern décor, they have grass-fed meats. She said this for Red's benefit, because he was a meat and potatoes man, which she had given up many years ago.

A waitress appeared, a young woman wearing a black apron over jeans and a white T-shirt. To Sharon's amazement, Red ordered for them, which he never has, not once, not that she remembers.

Bring us two green salads to start, both lightly dressed, with the goat cheese on the side, and for dinner, we'll split the striped bass, with an extra side of fries, well done, and a double helping of sautéed spinach. Lots of lemon, please. And another glass of wine for my wife, with the meal.

That should do us for now, yes? he asked.

Sharon nodded, and withheld comment about the discordant reference to the wife, too astounded that he recalled her tastes so well. Then again, he was all about the details.

Remember when we used to eat the daily catch in South Beach? he asked. *Melt in your mouth, right? Those were great holidays, way back when.*

All those fabulous deco buildings, the Latin beat and the food...

But not always warm.

No. Unreliable winters, I remember that too.

But we managed to stay warm.

She stiffened at the uncharacteristic nostalgia.

So. You're here, in Providence. First visit since I moved, and you want to talk about memory? Tell me, what's up?

Why does something have to be up?

Because, as you pointed out, we haven't been out to dinner for an age and you rarely travel beyond your borders these days, so, tell me. Getting married again? I would be happy for you, truly, just tell me.

That was a blip on the radar, Sharon.

Sorry to hear. So what then?

Well, I was thinking...

What?

I was thinking maybe enough time has passed.

Enough time for what?

To spend some time together.

He smiled, sheepishly, averting her gaze as she stared at him in disbelief.

What the hell are you talking about? We've known each other a long time, Red. You're here to tell me something important enough to make the trip. I can't believe I didn't connect the dots. What is it?

Maybe you don't know me as well as you thought.

Seriously?

Just a simple observation.

You don't do simple observations. You deconstruct the complex. So please, deconstruct, for me.

Can't I enjoy dinner with my ex-wife? Mother of my children.

Oh my God. The guessing game? I wasn't a fan all the years I had to extract what you were thinking and I've no patience for passive-aggression now. Please, Red. Spit it out!

A flush rose in his cheeks. He took a long gulp of wine. He sighed, nearly a groan, and hung his head like the kid who blew the play that lost the game. An unusual pose for an imposing man. She felt at once the knot in her stomach she always felt whenever he was distressed. When work was overwhelming or finances stretched, or when one of his partners succumbed too young to one of those killer cancers. She was usually able to read him, to recognize the emotion hidden below the stoicism and seldom visible to others, and she was always determined to make it right, often at her own expense, so she came to believe.

She repeated. *Spit it out. Definitely something I need to know, I see it now.*

Red leaned forward with a penetrating gaze. *All right, honey,* he said somberly. *Stage 3 lung cancer. 3B, in fact. Inoperable. Incurable. Enough spit for you?*

Sharon froze. She peered closely at him. She saw how pale he was under the flush and this would also explain the weight loss.

Tears sprang to her eyes. She reached for his hand, which he grasped tightly, gratefully. Tears also gathered along the rim of his eyes, something so rare it tore at her heart, and in those eyes, the joys, the challenges, and the setbacks of a lifetime together – the bonds of a marriage, albeit frayed, never fully shredded.

They sat in silence for a moment when, to Sharon's greater surprise, a surge of rage swelled. How dare he invade her carefully constructed life? How dare he bring this dark cloud to her door and elbow his way into the center of her universe again?

It's actually not as bad as it sounds, he said.

Sharon bristled. Oblivious, always, she thought. Never able to read her mood or her expression until she spelled it out, and then reacting like an innocent bystander. Even now he spoke in the tone of voice he often deployed in the midst of conflict, a tone meant to smooth things over. Reshape the debate. She withdrew her hand.

For the moment it's in…

Remission?

Not remission as much as submission, after one nasty round of chemotherapy, radiation too, and state of the art meds. Even the most virulent cancer tends to be tamed, for a time, but gone, no. Lurking, so to speak.

He poured wine into his glass and she noticed a slight tremor in his hand.

Are you in pain? She asked the right question, ever the dutiful wife, even as she had the urge to make a quick exit. Run from the first clap of thunder.

Not so much pain as a chronic ache, which I'm used to now. Could be much worse.

The waitress appeared with salads and another glass of white wine. She drained the last of Sharon's first glass into the second, to which Sharon might have objected if she were not in a controlled state. She hates to mix the tepid into the cold, the new with the old, but not the time to fuss.

He lifted his glass in a toast. *To a longer life than expected,* he said, and again she welled up with tears, and again with anger, for the unfairness of it, for him, and for her sons.

There must be a trial? Immunotherapy? Genetic engineering? This is a good time to be a guinea pig. I know a genomics professor, I'll ask her.

My doc is on top of it. He delights in talking about options while presenting my scans, tracing the erratic shapes. Reminds me of those cartoons, the ones where the dark ominous dictator of a fictional third world country looms over the smaller, the powerless. The tumor is a lesser evil now by virtue of size, not virility. Quietly deadly. Sort of like our marriage those last years.

This comment was a particular rarity and her instinct suggested defensive mode, but she refrained. Red rarely speaks of their demise and no point in this moment to revisit old terrain. What was Einstein's definition of insanity? Doing the same thing again and again, expecting a different outcome?

There must be another treatment? she asked.

Not yet.

I can't believe the boys don't know – you've just seen them. They don't know, right? she asked, although certain they would have called her, no matter an oath of silence.

I timed the visit for after treatment. And I'm already bald. He chuckled, sadly. *I hate they will have to deal with this. Maybe the worst part,* he said, sipping the wine and lowering his eyes.

She nodded sympathetically and, although she tenderly touched his arm, a reflex, a supportive gesture, the fury of a protective mother reared and roared.

If you had quit smoking thirty years ago when I begged you to. And twenty years ago. And ten years...

She had hounded him to quit because he promised he would when they married. A promise never kept. A violation of trust never recovered. She had grown increasingly intolerant of the smell of smoke on his clothes. An acrid taste on his lips. Middle of the night spasms. Scratchy breath and hoarse voice. And now, the inevitable diagnosis.

I wondered low long it would take you to go there. Frankly, I expected sooner. Well, I've quit now, for whatever that's worth. Too little too late, I know, but I have.

She briefly clung to her outrage, her dark blue eyes glaring into his paler blue, what he once described in a romantic moment as the dusk to his dawn.

Sorry, she murmured at last, with a heavy sigh. *I am, I'm sorry. Pointless now. Out of order.*

That expression, out of order, their code when the children's arguments went too far or when their own angry silences persisted.

I'll tell the boys next week, not that I'm looking forward to that. Would you come with me?

Will be good for you to have time alone with them. Not on the tennis court or watching football. Real time. Anyway, I'm midway through fall term and I can't take time off. With the sabbatical coming up, I have a lot on my plate. Spend time with them together. They'll meet you in Philly. Use the same subterfuge you used with me, business. Reserve a funky hotel. I'll be there in spirit, and if they want to see me, you'll spot them the fare, right?

Sure. Can't take it with me.

She was astounded by the finality of that remark. Her stomach churned. She forced herself to eat a few bites of salad and sipped the wine.

So, beyond serving as moral support, what can I do? she asked, as she reached for the basket of warm crusty bread on the table. She lathered butter over one slice and handed it to Red before buttering another.

Nothing like French butter, he said after the first bite. *Just the right ratio of salt to fat. People talk about bread all the time, they think it's the bread we crave and good bread is, of course, divine, in the truest sense of the word, but the bread is just a carrier, you know, for the butter. I'm talking real butter, the good stuff. Nothing like it.*

A smudge of butter clung to his upper lip and she lifted a hand to swipe it away, then refrained. How slowly habits pass, she mused. How little things change in the end, far less than she, than most women, she imagines, anticipate, especially when attempting to rid themselves of the shackles of a once sweet relationship turned sour.

How little changes in conversation as well. How many times has Red commented on the bread and butter equation? The sort of remark that plays well at a dinner party. She too was charmed, at first, until she grew weary of his chronic restatements of the obvious. Still, as she savored the bread and butter, she had to acknowledge the truth of it.

Red wiped his mouth, sat back and said, *since you've asked, there is something you can do for me.*

He had an unusually hangdog expression on his face and she was reminded of the day he unexpectedly brought home a puppy – a rare spontaneous moment that delighted the boys. Sharon was furious.

You should have asked first, she cried, because she knew the responsibility would fall to her. *Dogs have to be walked. They cannot be left alone too long.*

Her argument fell on deaf ears and as she watched Red and the boys frolic with the pup, the big man tumbling with the three kinetic creatures, she had to laugh. Another squabble ended by evasion. Years later, their most voluble disagreement over separation of assets had been the dog and because she wanted to put an end to the vitriol, she relinquished ownership. When the dog died, Red called to tell her and together they cried.

What can I do? she responded to his remark, more somber in this moment than angry.

Well, I was thinking... He paused again, like a toddler who cannot express his feelings.

What?

I was thinking, maybe we might...

My Lord, like pulling teeth. What?

I was thinking we might go away together. Someplace sunny and warm. We used to talk about being snowbirds, remember?

Dumbfounded again, she knocked on the tabletop. *Earth to Red! Have you noticed we're not married anymore?*

I know, I know, but I thought, maybe, since you're on sabbatical winter term, we might, I mean, we're divorced, but we're friends. And I'd like to spend time with you, while there is time. Somewhere different, not traveling down memory lane. Maybe a casita in Mexico, on the Pacific or the Oaxacan coast. I'll swim and fish, while you finalize your dissertation defense. I'll make sure you have good office space and reliable Internet. I'll grill the fish for dinner. We'll consume gallons of fresh sangria. I'll pay for everything. And the boys can come visit when they have time, so we can be together, all of us, now and then.

Sharon stared at him in disbelief and Red seized on the pause to press his case.

I thought we could just, you know, do what we never got to do because, well, we got so caught up in all that stuff. We never got to coast into old age.

You still think the failure of our marriage was stuff? Kids, work, menopause! Oh my God, I remember that conversation. What ruined the marriage was gross negligence. Divergent priorities. The steady dissolution of a relationship that was a mistake from the start.

A mistake, you say? That's a new one.

I'm sorry. I don't know where that came from.

Unfinished business, apparently. I had hoped we were beyond that. I had no idea you're still sifting through sand.

I'm not sifting anything. I've moved on. And now you bring all this to me, you bring it all back...

Mea culpa. He held up his hands, palms facing her to parody surrender, but she has seen this move before. A pose meant only to placate.

She stood, perhaps too quickly as she had to grab the chair to steady her wobbly legs. *Excuse me. I need a moment.*

He started to stand as well, but she gestured to him to stay seated, then turned and hurried to the restroom, where she had a rushed silent cry in the stall. She dabbed a damp paper towel under her eyes to sop up streaks of mascara. She scrubbed her hands with vanilla-scented liquid soap and slipped them into a ferociously loud dryer that echoed the rumbling in her stomach and, in the subsequent silence, the ache in her heart. She took deep breaths, so loudly, emphatically, a woman standing near asked if she was all right.

Yes, she murmured. *Thank you, just stuff, you know?*

Stuff. Yep, that sums it up. Stuff. The woman nodded in commiseration.

Sharon cautioned herself to stay calm. This was not the time for marital wrath. Certainly not dispassion. She must do better. After all, he's there to confide in her. He's come in person. He wants to spend time with her. Touching, even if opportunistic.

She was suddenly reminded of a conversation she'd had with her first new friend after the move, a calculus scholar who looked more like Nefertiti – sepia skin, a voluptuous body, with black wavy hair and fiery eyes. Her classes were always fully subscribed. She had just resumed teaching after a year of nursing her husband through cancer. She surprised Sharon with a confession that her marriage had years ago gone flat. They had drifted apart, staid was the word she used, but they planned joint sabbaticals to travel, hoping to rekindle their fire. The cancer diagnosis caught them off guard and, much to her surprise, she said, the disease restored the marriage.

Suddenly you're partners again. The daily proximity, the shared battle. Long talks to pass hard nights, middle of the night hot showers and afternoon naps. These things wear down defenses like river over rock. We listened to books on tape or I read aloud. We played endless games of Go. We made crazy playlists on Spotify and named them for philosophers. Before we knew it, without dialogue or drama, we fell in love again. His passing was all the more excruciating for it, but I'm glad we had the long good-bye.

The professor apologized for saddling Sharon with such an intimate disclosure.

Although women need to share these feelings. Otherwise we take everything on our own shoulders, right? And here's the thing – feelings age, as we do. We adapt. If we're lucky, we renew. On the other hand, cancer doesn't change anything in the past – only what's to come, the professor commented.

These were the words on Sharon's mind as she made her way back to the table.

Dinner had been served. Red stood to push in her chair and she waited for him to sit before she spoke.

Listen, I'm reeling from this. I'm heartbroken, I am, and I'm glad you came to see me. But my life is on track right now. I have no real shot at tenure, but I might secure a long-term contract and I will have my degree, at long last. And I have a whole life here. I have friends. I even date occasionally. Now, you show up, hit me with this awful news, and I want to be helpful, I do, but I cannot go away with you. Is there something more I should know? What did your brothers say?

I haven't told them yet.

Oh Red, this keeping everything to yourself. Hiding from the people who care most about you. Isn't this a good time to give that up?

I wanted to tell you first. I know, it's bizarre, but I felt, even now, when a life altering event comes along, a man tells his wife first. Maybe you could cut me a little slack? Maybe I never accepted our ending as easily as you.

Is it worse than you're admitting? Or are you here because you need a caregiver?

I don't need taking care of, not yet, and I won't ask that of you, Sharon.

Don't let the boys give up their lives either, although they will want to spend more time with you.

I know, I know. I cannot make all our lives about me. My blueprint. I remember that lecture.

He swallowed the last of his wine. *I see your new life hasn't tamed your temper.*

It's just, well, it's a lot to deal with all at once. You've had time with it. I need time now.

He sat back in his chair with a heavy sigh.

I see that. I do. But a thing like this, it knocks the guard down. I thought nothing could be worse than the separation, but this has sort of done me in.

Sharon nodded, astonished by his candor, and by the angst he has never before displayed. Perhaps the old dog has learned a few new tricks after all, she thought. *I'm glad you told me, in person.*

A strained silence settled between them, the same sort of silence they suffered during their last years together, when they lost their way. When there were no words left to say.

Red started to eat, then put his fork back down. *Let's face it, honey. I'm the same man you married. I never changed, you did. I know who I am. I'm an engineer, always in my head. Always in my orbit, as you said. Guilty. Ironically, an engineer is trained to expect the unexpected, less what is as what might result, but when something like this happens, when you're blindsided, like when you asked me for a divorce, I'm knocked off course with my compass stuck in place. I know I'm being selfish. That's who I am. That's the man you married. And you know that old saying – you don't get older, you get more so? Being sick, that's a whole other layer of more so. So you reach out for whatever you need. No, I don't need you to take care of me. I just want to be with you. We invested, what, thirty-eight, thirty-nine years in each other? There ought to be a better finish. Call me crazy.* He banged his palm against his head. *Maybe the cancer has already gone to my brain, but I was hoping for a few months together, hell I'll take a few weeks – no obligations and no commitments. You always loved a beach holiday.*

Forty years, Sharon muttered, and she was immediately sorry she said it.

Red laughed. *I knew I was off.*

She buried her face in her hands momentarily and when she looked up, Red was leaning so close she felt the heat of his breath.

How much pain are you in? Tell me true, she pleaded.

Not too bad. I've got potions and tinctures that ease the breathing. I've also got medical marijuana and

I've never slept so well. Might become a stoner in my old age.

That's it?

For the moment. Of course now I think those herbs may be hallucinatory.

He shrugged his shoulders with a boyish grin. Sharon remembers how taken she was with him that first date. She laughed at his anecdotes, admired his determination, and also, she had noticed at once, his inherent decency. When did she lose sight of all that?

Let's eat, smells delicious, he said, as he squeezed lemon generously over the fish and shook salt over the fries so aggressively the grains fell like hailstones.

Sharon picked at her meal as he devoured every morsel, after which he insisted they share a slice of apple pie, topped with a mound of whipped cream he lapped up contentedly.

Looks like your appetite has held up, she observed, despite the lesser bulk.

During the treatment, no, could barely keep anything down, but now everything tastes extra good.

In a matter of moments, only a few crumbs remained on the plate. Little left to say either.

I wish I could do something, Sharon murmured.

Red again took one of her hands and pressed it to his chest, over the tumor, she feared, and she felt the urge to pull back, to not cause him further harm.

Another dinner some time? Maybe a few?

Of course.

He raised his hand to signal for the check and after he settled the bill, they made their way to the exit.

I hate to say good-bye, he said.

She was struck by the sentiment. How she might have cherished that expression at the end of their marriage. Was it possible she might never see him again? Divorce feels so permanent when it happens, also surreal, but death? Non-existence? Unfathomable.

Shall we have an after dinner drink? Sharon suggested, surprising herself as well as Red.

Great idea.

They turned toward the bar and saw a young well-dressed couple vacating the stools where Sharon and Red sat earlier. The man said, *we saved these for you.* Red answered, *kind of you.*

Sharon watched the couple as they made their way to a table in the dining room.

A whole life ahead, Red commented.

She nodded and said, somberly, *a life filled with all sorts of surprises.*

The bar was noisy now, crowded with patrons dining as well as waiting for tables.

What's your pleasure? Amoretto or Tia? Red asked, speaking into her ear to be heard.

She laughed. These were their favorite liqueurs on winter holidays in tropical locations, toasting each day at the very end of the day.

A lifetime ago, she said.

BC, he chuckled.

Another code: Before Children.

She nodded. *Amoretto sounds good.*

He ordered and the bartender returned with tumblers filled with the sweet amber liqueur poured over one oversized ice-cube. They sat quietly, drinks cooling slowly over the cube like sand through an hourglass, as if the silence, the slowness, might suspend time. A great sadness settled over them both, beyond the distress of a death sentence: the sorrow between lovers who gave up on each other.

What does it matter how it plays out? Sharon thought. A lifetime together comes to an end one way or another.

They clinked and sipped. They smiled, grateful for the moment, for the space shared without words – words that might have been said, superfluous now.

Lines from a poem by Christina Rossetti came to Sharon's mind.

"And all the winds go sighing
For sweet things dying."

Red, she asked, her heart aching, her voice, and resistance, faltering. *Did you have a particular town in Mexico in mind?*

The Jaded Journalist

Early this Friday morning, a typically blustery morning in Northern California, the dance teacher arrived late to class. She is always late, I know, although I'm not one of her students. I am familiar with the class and with the teacher. In fact, I thought I knew her well.

When she arrives, the five mornings a week she teaches, she charges into the gym like a lightning bolt, yet she still stops to chat with a handful of regulars who have been working out with her for years, many since she launched the aerobic program thirty years ago in a smaller space before moving to the community center gym. After that, she pairs her iPhone to the Bluetooth speakers buried in the vaulted ceiling, dons a headpiece microphone like a rock star and checks the volume. These formalities delay the start time even longer and many students arrive late in defense.

I took a spot in back of the gym, to the side, to stay out of the way and minimize attention. Roughly fifty women, as young as twenty and as old as eighty, stood in clusters squawking like crows. Short and tall, large and small, most wore fashionable athletic apparel and sneakers with thick soles, while some, like me, wore oversized T-shirts and sweat pants, as if out for a walk. Towels, weights, mats and water bottles were scattered around the perimeter for easy access.

Several women nodded with barely concealed surprise. As the editor of the one town newspaper, I am often recognized. We exchanged scraps of small talk before they resumed their communal chatter, as essential to their morning rituals as coffee. They might have assumed I was there to write an article, although I profiled the dance teacher three years ago and the piece is still posted on a bulletin board in back.

I don't take fitness classes; however, now and then, I have peeked in to watch the throng of women hop and skip and shimmy to excessively loud music bursting from the rafters like a heady wind down the wide carpeted hallway and out the center's tall double doors. The dance routines, combinations of roughly a dozen basic moves, are choreographed to playlists of hip-hop, country, techno, classic rock and Latin music, not at all the sounds one expects to hear reverberating down the Main Street of a sophisticated suburb. Decibel levels and the pounding bass rival rap music emanating from the car radios of adolescents, rhythms orchestrated to awaken the psyche as well as the body. The crowd moves nearly in unison under stridently bright recessed lights, sneakers squeak along varnished floors, and many sing along with, to my mind, ridiculous songs exhorting suitors to *bring on the ring* and with street vernacular like *come get it, Bae,* as well as the more traditional lyrics admonishing ex-lovers for misdeeds or welcoming long summer days.

Dancers line up in rows, each occupying a small square of floor space, sufficient to move about and stretch out, but avoid collision, and when one goes right and the other left, and often crash, they laugh, because even though the workout is meant to be serious exercise, the intent is to have a good time. The dance teacher has been known to ponder aloud how anyone would rather run on a treadmill or spin on a stationary bike when they could dance.

I'm a runner. Four times a week, at daybreak, I jog for an hour or so. I'm rarely plugged in and silence the phone to clear my mind or review thoughts in my head that will translate to content. The exact opposite of jumping, sidestepping or kickboxing, and swishing hips in tempo to a voice shouting instructions over raucous music.

This dance teacher, whose classes are always packed, maintains a running commentary on the latest episode of *Dancing with the Stars* or *The Voice*, reality television I abhor, but which seems to rally the crowd, and she regales them with anecdotes of her adolescent daughters, intrusive in-laws or vacations run amok. The dancers love it. For one hour, global strife, politics and personal struggles are in check, the syncopation of snaps, taps and treads echoing the escalating beat of their hearts, until they return to daily living.

I get the appeal, just not for me.

When I wrote the profile for the newspaper, I learned, although I didn't appreciate the significance at the time, that the dance teacher's followers seem devoted to her as much or more than the dance, even more than the prospect of trimmer bodies – she a Queen Bee to their hive. The sheer banality of her life, I think, is akin to reality television, infusing her with an exalted status among disciples.

I failed then to grasp the complexity of their relationship, largely because I tend to be a snob about franchised frivolity. I never peeked beyond the bright lights and spandex to the heart of the story.

In the end, I committed the journalist's worst offense: I didn't just bury the lede – I missed it entirely. As a seasoned reporter and longtime editor-in-chief, I should have known better.

In my defense, I might have been short of space when I published her profile or, more likely, pressed for time. One of my three children was still living at home and I produce the 32-page *Weekly Times* almost single-handedly. Like similar newspapers across the country earning barely enough revenue, largely through real estate and retail advertising, to stay afloat, little is left over after paying the printer and my meager salary. I contract a stringer or photographer only when there's spare change. There is no dedicated office either. I work from home or at one or another café in town where patrons have been known to share gossip or add perspective to a story. Locals love to be quoted and they want to be heard. Several of them regularly submit wordy letters to the editor and sometimes the hardest part of my job is choosing which to include and which to decline in favor of keeping the peace.

Our readers also relish profiles of residents, especially celebrities or sports stars, or those whose work has become a cornerstone of the community. For this reason, when the national Dancercise Company issued a press release three years ago announcing its 30th anniversary, I arranged to meet with the dance teacher. Longevity itself is an achievement, even if I look down my nose at what seems to me bourgeois.

We met that day at a popular coffee house. She arrived a little late, straight from class, flushed and breathless, casting a youthful glow, although she had recently turned fifty and puffy gray bags under her eyes suggested a perpetual lack of sleep. She drank one double latté followed by one coffee refill.

I never get enough, she said with a sly smile, as if confessing a sin, *although I know when I've had enough.*

She was a deceptively simple subject, one of those maddeningly cheerful people with the energy and figure of a cheerleader. She joked about having to dance her way to the grave to compensate for an addiction to potato chips. She proudly described how she had come to acquire one of the first Dancercise franchises in the country and over the years cultivated and trained recruits to teach the evening classes. When I asked why she only teaches mornings, she said something innocuous about getting a head start on the day. I didn't pursue the point. When she checked her watch several times and I asked if she was rushed, she said, *no, just one of those people always watching the clock.* This did not jive with her reputed tardiness, but I let that pass as well.

She mentioned having three children, although subsequently spoke only of the two daughters who occasionally, reluctantly, she said, join her at class. *Guess there won't be Dancercise and Daughters*, she joked. This I quoted.

She told me the organization, what she referred to as corporate, had recently sent her a video of one of her early classes. *Around 1992, although I have no memory of that dance, or the song. I definitely don't remember the outfit, which was outrageous.* She giggled like a schoolgirl. *My husband would remember exactly what he was wearing then because he's still wearing it!*

She giggled again in that way people who resist judgment laugh at themselves. Is it no wonder I didn't take her seriously?

To my surprise, when the interview came to a close, she asked about my husband.

Please send him my very best, she said, with a curious expression in her eyes, as if wondering if I knew something I did not. I had no idea they were acquainted and when I'd mentioned that morning I was meeting with her, my husband did not comment.

You know Jack? I asked.

She smiled like the cat that swallowed the canary. *Yes. So smart, so kind. I like the way he talks, like a regular person, you know?*

I had to laugh. Many people idealize physicians, particularly an esteemed neurologist like Jack, as if medical rock stars, and I made a mental note to tease him about it. However that night, when I passed along the dance teacher's regards, he was notably circumspect.

You know I can't talk about her, he said. *Patient confidentiality.*

We were sitting at the dinner table and as he sipped red wine, he gazed into his glass the way a fortuneteller gazes into a crystal ball.

I'm not asking you to discuss a patient, I snapped. *Just having a little fun with how impressed she was with you. Is,* I corrected myself, remembering she spoke in present tense.

I would have dismissed the conversation then and there, except for the wistful expression on Jack's face. A subtle knitting of the brow and downcast eyes. The way people appear when reminded of someone significant who, for reasons beyond their control, has been lost to them.

Jack is a wonderful man and we are a good couple. Thirty-two years of marriage attests to that. I supported him through medical school as a cub reporter and he supported me when all the children were in school and I took a few years to earn a master's degree. He is also my most trusted reader. Every week he reviews the pre-press edition, never one to ignore an opportunity to question a detail, set me straight on what he considered misrepresentation, or correct the typo or word gaffe no one else would notice. When he subsequently commented on the profile of the dance teacher, he was curiously critical of the piece as a whole.

You gave her short shrift. You skimmed the surface, he scolded.

In truth, which my husband surely supposed, I went into the interview believing there was not much beyond the surface. No reason to, in light of benign comments from those I interviewed, who spoke of her good humor and hubris, her devotion to the cause, etc. Nothing piqued my interest.

When I bristled at his reproach, he became more vociferous in her defense.

You wrote her off because she never finished college. Because she dedicates herself to a class of gentrified women with punishing body images prancing around to the same radio soundtrack the vast majority of people, those not devoted to NPR, tune into while driving.

He knows me well. I am unapologetically smug about a culture I believe has been dumbed down, aided and abetted by 24/7 television and social media. On the other hand, I am not disinterested in dance, not artistic dance – I am simply more interested in the literary and fine arts. I attend modern dance performances now and then and, as a girl, my mother occasionally took my sisters and I to the ballet, which she considered crucial, like theater and the symphony, to a solid education. My father preferred jazz, also musical theater. He sang along loudly with Rogers and Hart or Cole Porter songs and I have fond memories of him when, on occasion, after dinner, after a scotch or two, when he heard what he called finger-snapping music on the radio, he turned up the volume, grabbed my mother and swept her across the living room, deftly avoiding furniture, leading her in a lindy or waltz they must have enjoyed during courtship and reserved in later years for family weddings or the annual spring festival. I sat in the corner watching their shoulders and hips dip and sway, tapping my toes to the rhythm and practicing the steps afterward in my room, much like the women who practice in the gym.

I defended the profile by insisting that I was appropriately reverent. I described to readers that the dance teacher had dropped out of a state university in her junior year because she was bored, she said, as well as daunted by the challenge of a career on the stage. She used the last of her tuition savings, and convinced her rookie lawyer husband to invest, to purchase one of the first franchises of a novel fitness program based on popular dance. She owns four of them now, spanning neighboring towns in Marin County, an affluent suburban enclave serving San Francisco. Instructors across the country celebrate her tenure and she has thousands of followers on Facebook. She told me three hundred members pay a modest monthly fee for the privilege of attending any of the eleven weekly classes. Including drop-in charges, I estimated her gross earnings at well over a quarter-million dollars.

I applauded her aplomb, and her success, I argued, in an effort to uphold the legitimacy of an admittedly skimpy profile. *I penned an accurate sketch: fitness entrepreneur, wife, mother, television addict, chronic dieter and raconteur. That's the story.*

He sighed with exasperation and I realized then there was something he knew that he might have told me, but chose not to, and this exacerbated the nagging thought there was more to their relationship.

That night, after the newspaper went to press, I dug up the recording of the interview with the dance teacher and heard a disclosure that might have been mined. She said dance is a symbiotic relationship.

We never dance alone, even if it seems we do. Dancing bonds us. The music comes through us and from us. People think I'm the one charging their batteries, but the truth is, they're charging mine.

I should have quoted this or I should have asked for clarification, but I was too busy rushing through the interview. Jack was right. The profile was two-dimensional. The sort of journalism I rail against – no real reporting, rather restating the obvious.

For weeks after the article was published, the possibility of a relationship between my husband and the dance teacher gnawed at me. I had to fight off an acute fear of infidelity, the apprehension of a post-menopausal female facing increasingly discernable sags and wrinkles and an erratic libido. More to the point, anyone as perpetually cheerful as the dance teacher, one who complains of only minor nuisances like lackadaisical daughters or a sister-in-law who brings inedible food to Thanksgiving, that woman would be particularly attractive to a man saddled with an uncompromising wife.

Still, I buried the thought, dismissing anxiety in favor of trust, and we never spoke of it again until the other day, after I ran into the dance teacher and finally got the story.

I was at a corner table at the café where I often spend Wednesday mornings working on the pre-press layout. The owner favors classical background music, rather than more common intrusive Pandora rock or techno playlists, which is more amenable to wrangling content on a laptop.

It was late morning, after the breakfast crowd and before lunch, so the café was largely empty. I looked up when I noticed two people paused at the doorway. I did not, at first, recognize the dance teacher. It has been three years, and also a totally different context. Not unusual. Instructors, waitresses, nurses, familiar in place, barely exist outside their milieu, and she looked particularly different out of uniform. She wore a cropped sky blue sweater that skimmed her hips, and faded jeans, like a graduate student. Black ankle boots with a short stacked heel made her taller, also more statuesque. Her wavy blonde hair, freed from the confines of the ponytail she wears to class, cascaded gently to her shoulders, and layers of blush and blue eye shadow completed her, as if she arrived each morning to dance class as a sketch and in the light of day converted into the finished work of art.

She peered around the café like a secret service agent. She didn't acknowledge me; she might not have recognized me either. Behind her stood a tall husky adolescent boy. She gripped his hand and led him tentatively forward and I saw at once he was not quite right. His head tilted, his stance seemed off kilter and despite the shadow of stubble along the jawline, he had the dark frightened eyes of a child.

Autistic. The word came to mind instantly, although I had only once encountered an autistic child, the son of old friends whose lives were forever altered by his limitations. Much has been published in the press in recent years about an increasing incidence, including the accusatory rhetoric against vaccinations as a possible culprit. I read recently the AMA revised the diagnostic terminology, which previously included Asperger's Syndrome, to delineate all forms of Autism on a spectrum, suggesting, I hope, position on a continuum means greater opportunity to progress, although more likely for purposes of treatment.

The only time the subject had come on the radar of the newspaper was at a PTA meeting last year, in an argument having to do with the cost of special education. I interrogated parents who complained they have to convey special needs kids to schools beyond the town border at exorbitant personal expense, and others who bemoaned the increasing imbalance in funding between special education and enrichment programs like the arts. I wrote about budget woes.

Years ago, I read a novel about a captivating autistic boy and there have been caricatures of the savant on film, something else entirely. Otherwise I'm uninformed, like most of us, purposely blind in that there-but-for-the-Grace-of-God mantra.

The dance teacher guided the boy to the counter and ordered. His body swayed on large feet anchored to the floorboards. He wore baggy jeans and a T-shirt embellished with a silver graphic of the band Metallica. When they sat at a table facing me, I was able to observe better and recognized the familial features. No question he was the son she mentioned only once as part of the family line-up.

I felt an immediate sense of despair, for her, for all the parents of compromised children. Jack and I weathered a few storms with our kids, but none bore genetic constraint. The oldest has a short fuse and from the first resisted authority, so we were often called to conference with his teachers to try to shed light on what we believed was merely a bright mind in an irascible personality. A boy, Jack argued eloquently, requiring patience, not condemnation. He ultimately worked out his aggressions on the playing field and in high school developed a fondness for beer, then settled down. The youngest found her passion in poetry, also promiscuity, which necessitated endless dialogue and oversight. She has a ferociously feminist spirit, which I admire. Our middle daughter, a pleaser, is pursuing a doctorate in early childhood education and I expect she will be an extremely empathetic educator. They all had their share of tussles and torment, and many tearful moments, as did Jack and I, but we never questioned their ability to evolve into fully functioning adults.

I watched as the dance teacher leaned forward in her chair toward her son. She murmured to him in a low voice as she screwed off the cap on a bottle of orange juice, which he chugged all at once. The owner delivered plates overflowing with omelets and roasted potatoes, with a supportive pat on the dance teacher's back. As the boy devoured his meal, she leaned back in her chair, a brief respite, and then dived into her own. Between bites, she sipped a tall iced cappuccino.

The town's silver haired retired librarian walked in and placed her order. She nodded to me and to the dance teacher, sweetened her iced tea, and took a seat outside under a table umbrella, where she opened a fat plastic-coated library book with obvious delight.

The only patrons inside now, the dance teacher focused on her son and I, distracted from my work, on their pas de deux.

All at once, the boy stood, looming over his mother, and with a growl, upended the table. Her breakfast plate and the plastic container slid down to her lap. She sat very still. No reaction. Remarkable composure, considering the disruption and the mess.

Then she swept off the detritus on her body, stood and eased slowly closer to her son, whose arms and hands wildly punched the air around him. To my mind, decidedly threatening.

She didn't touch him. She waited a moment and then whispered into his ear. He snarled. He shook his head back and forth as she continued to murmur, as if they were the only two people on the planet. She placed one hand on his shoulder as gently as a butterfly landing and the boy slowly, visibly, deflated, until he hung his head, trembling still, but far less agitated. She took his elbow and steered him to sit, resumed her seat opposite and wiped off what remained of the food and drink on her clothes. After a few moments, assured, I imagined, he was no longer volatile, she made her way to the register to order an oatmeal cookie, which, I surmised by the boy's glee, may have been the source of the skirmish. Perhaps she hoped to minimize sugar or maybe the cookie was meant to be a reward, but he wanted it now – an impulsive toddler in the body of a grown man.

As she turned from the register to deliver his treat, she noticed me and smiled. I returned the smile, but made no effort to engage her in conversation, although the mother of an autistic son of his age must have inured herself long ago to embarrassment when such commotions occur. I admired her determination not to make her son a prisoner at home, or wherever he resided, and to face the fate of an outing at a local café for the sake of his socialization, as well as her own, whatever the repercussions.

Over dinner that night, I told Jack about the incident and he nodded knowingly. I realized then the family must have consulted with him. I felt humbled by his silent support and this time, when I saw the pensive expression on his face, I recognized the humility there. What I saw in his eyes was the curse of the physician confronted with a condition he cannot comprehend, much less cure.

Whatever my husband might have felt for the dance teacher, whatever bond they may have forged, I knew I had disappointed him, and I was disappointed in myself, having clung to the high ideals journalists expound without living up to them.

What am I reporting? I cried with exasperation. *The dean said I had unflinching observational insight, remember? He said I would win a Pulitzer. And what do I write? I write gobbledygook about sewer repairs bogging down traffic. The debate over parking lots or Starbucks. School board scuffles. Budget battles. Stuff and nonsense! And a woman runs an independent business, as vain glorious as it seems to me, while raising a severely handicapped son, and this I miss entirely. How did I not even know? It's a small town. I'm the chief reporter and I never got a whiff.*

You were on assignment. You wrote about the dance franchise. Her son has nothing to do with that, and she never said a word in the interview, right? Perhaps she wanted to protect his privacy as she cannot protect him from prying eyes. Maybe she deserved her moment in the sun. Wasn't that the story you were after? That should be the presiding editorial principle – stay on topic. Sorely needed in this era, I'd say.

I'm a reporter, Jack, not ruled by confidentiality. I'm supposed to get the whole story.

And I'm saying not every story must be told.

He was right, of course. I spent a sleepless night questioning my fitness for journalism and my role as a voice for truth. By morning, this Friday morning, I decided to skip my run and instead drove to town to dance class. I hoped I might engage the dance teacher on this subject. Pen a feature piece on autism worthy of its significance and make up for my failure to get the more important story.

So there I stood in the gym, awaiting dance class with the crowd of chatty regulars.

Sunlight filtered through tall Palladian windows, casting half-moon shadows across the floor, and anticipation filled the air, although, despite the buzz and light, the room came to life only when the dance teacher arrived. She mounted the elevated platform, added during renovations a few years ago to accommodate an occasional speaker, a panel discussion or play reading, or the overflow from a controversial city council meeting in the adjacent town hall.

The perfect spot for an instructor to model the dance moves and, five mornings a week for an hour or so, feel the commander of her fate.

This morning, even multi-colored leggings and a hot pink spandex top she wore like a second layer of skin failed to mask a heavy heart. Her whole body seemed to sag as she set up, without a word, and then she said, in an uncharacteristically subdued voice, *let's begin.*

I wasn't the only one who noticed. The regulars up front stepped forward together toward the stage like an honor guard and a hush fell over the room.

Whatever the source, women recognize at once the signs of heartbreak. Instincts far better tuned than the best journalist. The way a hummingbird zeroes in on nectar or a bee zooms in on lavender, it's the radar we share, crossing class, culture and context. Our reaction, alternately supportive or defensive, was today, distinctly protective.

The dance teacher pulled her shoulders back and lifted her head. Her legs settled firmly to the platform. To a mournful ballad by Rhianna, she steered the class to stretch from heads to toes, prepping for the aerobic moves to come. And then, midway through the first dance, a bouncy rock tune by Bruno Mars, she stumbled. The crowd gasped as she slumped to her knees and paused, before looking up apologetically, and I saw in her expression the burden mothers take on for that which they bear no blame.

I'm so sorry, she whimpered, her apology echoing through the speakers, rippling over and through each of us.

Just one of those nights, she added, shrugging her shoulders with a half-smile. She stood. *I really need you guys today.*

And there it was – the symbiosis she mentioned in the interview I failed to cite. The real story: a teacher who draws the strength she needs to cope with a challenging family life from her students, even as they believe they derive their energy from her.

The crowd stirred. They all whooped and applauded. The dance teacher restarted the music and resumed her place at the center of the stage. A broad smile spread over her face as she called out the first cue to the dance and, in that moment, I thought it best to show my solidarity by dancing.

The Disbelieving Daughter

When Deana returned from a brisk 8-mile run Saturday morning, she found a FedEx envelope on her doorstep, and inside that envelope, a smaller envelope from the Star of David Cemetery in Connecticut, and inside that, like nesting Russian dolls, a letter informing her that her mother, Ruth, who died ten years ago, was never buried. The casket had been recently discovered pressed against the back wall of a secondary vault, a cold storage locker where cadavers are stowed in the depth of winter until the earth is malleable for digging – a few days, perhaps a few weeks – when the dearly departed can be descended into their eternal graves.

Deana stood, shocked and shivering, in the vestibule of her townhouse, despite leggings and a fleece jacket and a tight fitting knit cap that captured most of her curly hair, wrapped sufficiently against the weather, not memory.

An image immediately came to mind: the last sight of her mother, the morning of the funeral, before the coffin was closed for the service. Deana had requested one last moment alone with her dead mother, which she regretted in the end. Ruth was sheathed in the obligatory white. Her face without the make-up she usually wore and hair slicked back, made her appear unusually severe, not at all the expression of serenity she had expected. A static pose, the lack of breathing, suddenly incomprehensible. With a deep sigh, Deana tucked a family photo under her mother's folded hands and replaced her wedding ring on her ring finger, then quickly pulled away, shaken by the unresponsiveness, the iciness, her mother Ruth known for steadfastness and decorum, not stillness.

She read the letter again, scanning the words as if she might have missed something, or misunderstood, and while she read, behind her eyes, her mother's face morphed into a familiar expression of dissatisfaction, displeased with Deana and, to a lesser extent, her brother, Leonid, for this outrageous situation.

Trudging into the house on wobbly legs, Deana felt wearier from the weight of the message than the running. She removed her jacket and cap and hung them on a hook by the door, tossed her keys into the blue pottery bowl on the foyer table, and made her way down the hall to the kitchen, where she placed letter and phone on the round breakfast table, where crusts of toast and shreds of scrambled egg clotted on her breakfast plate. She poured the last of the tepid coffee from her thermal mug into the sink and added the last of the warm from the pot. The mug trembled in her hand and her legs too shook perceptively, rattled by the missive, as if Ruth had only today passed away and her daughter had failed to fulfill her final wishes.

Absurd, Deana chided herself as she glanced at the wall clock, calculating the best time to call her brother.

The winter Deana's mother died had arrived early and lasted long. Frigid air pierced the damp earth, forcing a deep freeze from early December until the warming April rains. The funeral service had been held at the synagogue where Ruth was active all her adult life, one of many similar temples in a stretch of suburbs north of New York City along the eastern edge of the Hudson River. Deana had just turned thirty-five and Leo, thirty-two. They hoped the humbleness of the plain pine casket might make up in some way for the indignities Ruth had suffered the eighteen months she battled cancer. She was still young, sixty-seven years old, although she seemed older, she had always seemed older, like a classically stoical Chekhovian elder, the result of dark deep-set eyes, hair tucked behind her ears and a chiseled face fixed in an enigmatic gaze.

Deana barely attended the Rabbi's speech at the service, she hardly made sense of the eulogies given by her uncle and her mother's closest friend, and she even found it difficult to concentrate on her brother Leo's tribute, although the audience chortled repeatedly as he evoked his mother's endearing eccentricities.

Most of you know she delivered warm cookies to the rabbis every Friday morning. A generous gesture, of course, although, in private, she confessed the sweets were an effort to secure influence. The crowd chuckled knowingly. *She claimed she hated committees, then she managed to take over every committee she joined, and insisted all meetings were held at our house, volunteers packed into our tiny living room and then herded into the kitchen for the ritualistic pouring of red wine, my mother toasting to mission accomplished as she issued commands for next steps before the next meeting.* Hilarity rippled through committee members in the audience. *And, let us not forget, the early winter mornings, every year, when she piled the gently used blankets she extracted from many of you to present to the local homeless, even as she urged them to get help and get off the streets.* The whole congregation laughed and Deana nodded in affirmation. *No point to self-pity* was one of her mother's many familiar reprimands. Also, *no good deed goes unpunished.*

Today, in the face of this folly, Deana thought she might find consolation in her mother's mantras. Ruth would feel less anger than incredulity at this crazy turn of events. She was far more accepting than the prototypical Jewish mother, and more tolerant than Deana, treating most everything in her path with good humor and a sense of inevitability. Fate, Ruth alleged, is the definitive escort, even as she contended that destiny is in each individual's hands.

The Rabbi, in his remarks at the funeral, expressed his respect for her constancy. He called her resolute. Formidable. Indomitable. And, the ultimate acclaim: devoted. Devotion, to Ruth, and her peers, a quality to admire and aspire to, as she often advised her daughter, a quality Deana's generation, the new wave feminists, denounce as subjugation.

Deana recalls now an exhortation the Rabbi made to mourners at the close of his comments, the one thing a rabbi has ever said that provoked serious contemplation.

What we all must consider, what you must learn to make meaning of your life, and which Ruth understood, is this: what is the question to which your life is the answer?

Deana has yet to figure that one out.

Soon after the funeral, Leo moved away and Deana returned to her busy life. One year later, they rejoined at the cemetery plot, where the Rabbi recited the ritual prayer to mark the official end of mourning and the unveiling of the headstone. That was that, so they believed. Death acknowledged and rituals honored. No reason to question otherwise.

Deana was struck the day of the unveiling, as she was at her father's unveiling three years earlier, by the irony of this Jewish tradition. Just as grief subsides, family members are obligated to convene at the burial site; however, rather than closure, the ceremony dredges up the loss. One of many religious customs she fails to comprehend.

Ruth's unique question most surely was this: *how can we make people's lives a little easier?* An immigrant woman who delighted in good news and good people, she subjugated herself to no one. She graduated from the City College of New York with a major in European literature and a lifelong affection for writers Tolstoy and Pushkin.

Russian through and through, Deana's father used to remark, both scold and satisfaction.

Ruth had no illusions about writing as a vocation, she was far too practical, nor any intention of spending her life as a secretary. She wanted to be an editor, but soon discovered, to her everlasting chagrin, the affluent graduates of women's colleges claimed the coveted editorial positions at publishing houses as well as magazines. Determined to earn an income, she took a position in the customer service department at Macy's, where she remained over forty years, rising to manager, until the cancer treatment weakened her so severely she was unable to do her job to her own exacting standards.

Every workday, during her lunch hour, the one hour she called her own, she read classic literature she borrowed weekly from the library, which seemed to suffice.

Deana scanned the letter again. How would her mother handle this customer service fiasco? And where was her almighty God when she was shoved to the back of cold storage to languish a decade?

At last, Deana called Leo. She was still sitting at the breakfast table, still in sweaty clothes, still stunned. Talking to her brother would help, it always helped. Leo lived in Paris with his husband Eric, whom he met when he moved there, shortly after Ruth's death, and after several years in a civil union, they wed, and now seemed to Deana one of few happily married couples she knew.

You cannot be serious, Leo replied after a moment of shocked silence and called out to Eric to share the news.

Holy shit! Eric shouted loudly. *That's insane.*

How could that even happen? Leo asked. *And, wait, when we were at the unveiling, she wasn't there?*

Apparently not.

And nothing seemed strange last time you were at the cemetery?

I never go. What would seem strange anyway?

You have never gone out there to visit?

Why would I drive fifty miles to stand in front of a cold engraved slab and a layer of grass?

People do, you know. I mean that's why they're there and not in an urn.

They're not in an urn because Jews do not cremate, not by choice, you know that. While I'm sure it gives some people comfort to visit a gravesite, not me.

Leo paused, never certain he truly understood his sister, although he would battle to the death to defend her right to think and do whatever she chose to think and do, because he practiced the golden rule, their mother's most recurrent mantra: *to each their own.*

What great irony it was, more than twenty years ago, a slap in the face, Leo said at the time, when Ruth found it so hard to accept her son's own.

You don't think I dropped the ball somehow D, do you? Leo asked. *The headstone was right, all to spec.*

No, no. I just cannot believe they never dug the grave and a year later put up the stone over nothing. Unless...

Unless what?

What if they buried someone else in mom's place?

Deana gasped, and when Eric made ghostly sounds in the background, Leo laughed.

Oh, this is SO not funny, Deana cried with irritation, as if they were adolescents, Leo taunting her when she slipped on an icy sidewalk on the walk to school or when she applied lipstick for her first date.

The thought of a stranger in her mother's place made Deana's heart heavier and Leo must have felt the same, as he abruptly stopped laughing.

I'll talk to them. You think we need a lawyer?

Deana knew she would have to be the one to take care of this. Leo was a successful architect with a revered European firm, about to embark on a high profile project. He had a husband who deserved his attention. Deana's marriage had ended five years ago and she has few obligations beyond her work as a business development consultant.

In truth, despite several active projects and a staff of twenty, she often has time on her hands.

I hope we don't need a lawyer, she sighed. *Let me talk to them and sort this out.*

We're on our way to Zurich, first thing in the morning, but I'll have all my screens. As you know, and Eric will attest, I always have my eyes on my screens. And D, we also need to arrange a service.

A service?

The cemetery was supposed to arrange for a rabbi to say Kaddish. Ours or one of their contingent. A minyan too, I think, at graveside. Mom would die if that did not happen. They shared a moment of silence to acknowledge the absurdity of that comment. *So, maybe the Rabbi never got the call, unless Eric is right, unless someone else is buried there.*

Jesus, this gets more bizarre by the moment.

Jesus has nothing to do with this.

Very funny.

You know, there is a silver lining. Jews believe the dead should have a companion until burial so, surrounded by ten years worth of stiffs, Mom has had plenty of company.

Deana cringed at the word stiff and she felt again the loss of her mother's steady hand as well as a mounting uneasiness that all the most important decisions she has made since her mother's death are deeply flawed. Is it possible Ruth has been trapped in a state of limbo all these years, watching her daughter butcher family values and make a mess of her life? She shuddered at the possibility, the specter of her mother's expression of displeasure rising again before her eyes.

I'll get to the bottom of this and figure out what needs to be done.

What a mess, D. Sorry I'm not there, not like you haven't had enough on your plate. Settled back home now?

Yes, finally, and renovation is past tense.

Happy with it?

Looks great, thanks again, your advice was perfect, as always.

Send more pics. We're hoping to get back some time soon, although this project will take a few years.

Maybe I'll get there sooner than you'll get here.

Stay longer next time.

I'll try.

Dare I ask, anyone new?

No one of interest.

Not like you to be single so long.

Maybe my time is up.

Don't be ridiculous. Won't be long now.

I appreciate your faith.

I just know you, D.

Deana laughed and it felt good to laugh. *Yes, you do.*

Did you happen to notice that Jason published something groundbreaking? Over my head, but big.

How do you know?

I'm still on his mailing list. Ever hear from him?

After all this time? He barely spoke to me in the end, you know that.

He was a jerk.

He's not. He's a good guy who married the wrong girl.

He told you to fuck off, as I recall, on the way out the door, so he's a jerk.

He had good cause.

Honey, it takes two to tango and you're my sister, so he's a jerk.

Deana fought back tears, uncertain whether she was overwhelmed by the memory of how badly she had wronged her husband or her brother's unwavering compassion, and she was certain Leo would know what she was feeling as more sensitive brothers recognize telltale conversational pauses.

To avoid any further discussion of a subject she had hoped to bury by now, she bid a hasty goodbye.

She stared at the letter in her hand, which was dated a month ago and had been forwarded from her last address, the home she shared for six years with Jason, a genetics research scientist with a winsome smile and an innate desire to please. When they met, Deana had come to terms with permanently solo status and he was the sort of man determined to settle down. In truth, she found it more comfortable, and exciting, to move from one relationship to the next, habitually coupled, also habitually fickle: a woman who desired romance over sustenance.

Ruth had been especially fond of Jason. She was taken with the nobility of his calling and his genteel demeanor. Deana too admired his high-mindedness. His equanimity. And she knew he loved her, although she wondered if he admired her more than adored her, which she feared was not sustainable. To her surprise, Jason shared her apprehension. The night before the wedding, he offered her an exit.

A one time get out of jail card, he said. *We both know you will tire of me.*

Deana felt in that moment as if glass might have been smashed, like a window in a locked attic on a steamy summer day shattered in order to capture a breath of air. She had only to crawl through that window and climb from the roof to freedom.

Instead, determined to be better than she was, she replied, *isn't it the bride who's supposed to have the wedding eve jitters?*

She also understood the marriage might be her last chance to settle down, if not for herself, for her parents, longing for grandchildren. In the end, she continued taking birth control, lacking faith in her constancy as well as the relationship.

Deana had never asked her mother for advice and only once asked her opinion, after she became, as Jason predicted, bored by their life together.

They were seated in the oncologist's anteroom waiting to discuss proposed treatment for the late-stage cancer. Classical music played in the background –

violins and a cello, no wind instruments or tympani – to underscore the somber scenario. A cloying artificial lavender scent emanated from a diffuser, clogging Deana's breath. She already expected the worst and Jason, in an especially gloomy mood that morning, bemoaned the absence of medicine to save his beloved mother-in-law.

The science is there, it's just too slow, he whimpered.

It's not about you, Deana snapped.

As she sat with her mother, annoyed with Jason, also annoyed with herself for not appreciating his intent, she asked her mother what she believed was the secret to a happy marriage. Ruth was surprised by the question, surely her daughter might have asked sooner, but Deana always thought of herself as so inherently different that Ruth could not possibly provide relevant guidance. She's not sure they had ever agreed on anything, although they rarely argued, and, to Ruth's credit, she never said a word about the absence of grandchildren. Jason described them once as a Venn diagram, operating in tandem, intersecting regularly, but only in shared space.

Ruth briefly contemplated the question. She typically gathered her thoughts before commenting, making her response all the more penetrating.

Reduce your expectations some, she answered. *Works all sorts of miracles.*

Deana was shocked by her response, but had to table the discussion to meet with the doctor. When she filled Leo in later that day on the prognosis and treatment plan, she also repeated their conversation.

Why is it better to reduce expectations? Isn't there something fundamentally wrong with lowering the bar simply to avoid failure? We were raised to always do better, right? What's the point of winning a slower race?

She imagined this might be particularly meaningful to Leo, who lent his voice and considerable financial support to the movement to legalize gay marriage. *No one gives up when so much is at stake,* he told Deana at the time.

Perhaps people give up only what is easily won, and she fears now she let her brother down most of all by allowing her marriage, so easily come by, to fail.

Six years ago, when Leo and Eric flew to New York to marry, Deana hosted their celebration. When the festivities had come to an end, guests gone, spouses asleep, Deana, under the influence of an excess of champagne, and wine, confided that her marriage was in the dumper and rather than face the music, she had been unfaithful.

For years, she whimpered shamefully. *And now, when I can sleep at all, I wake up gasping for air, as if I've been buried alive.*

Anyone I know? Leo inquired, with a drunken giggle.

Deana, grateful to confess without derision, described her first affair with the handsome realtor who sold them their house, their liaisons in homes staged for sale where the dread of discovery proved seductive. When that novelty wore off, she fell into bed with a linguistics expert she consulted with on a project. He followed Ayn Rand's philosophy and claimed the height of altruism was to ensure her sexual satisfaction. Despite continuous pleasure, she tired of his single-mindedness. Some time later, despite efforts to resist, she embarked on an affair with a philosophy professor who preached in class the obligation to the classicists' moral imperative, while bedding a married woman. She soon detested his lack of integrity only slightly more than her own.

You know, D, you have a fanatical fear of the banal, Leo observed that night. *Maybe marriage just isn't for you. On the other hand, promiscuity is a slippery slope. The new gets old soon enough.*

No open marriage for you guys?

For some, sure. For us, no. We waited too long to risk what we've got.

What a concept, Deana muttered.

My dear beautiful sister, what is it you want that you cannot seem to find?

Deana exploded in laughter, an intoxicated manic hilarity that ended up in tears, and Leo too descended into hysterics.

Mom would be furious with me, Deana blathered.

No honey, I'm the loser in this family, Leo said.

I guess we've both made a mess of it. Mom must be rolling in the grave.

This Saturday morning, the letter still in hand, Deana has the deeply disturbing sensation her mother is angrier with her for vacating her vows than with Leo for his marriage.

She shook herself off and took a long shower, changed into clean comfy clothes and slumped on the couch to call the cemetery, but she was reminded by an automated response that a Jewish graveyard is closed on Sabbath and administration would reopen Monday. To avoid full-on misery, she pulled out her notes on a project. She enjoyed her work. She liked the many moving parts. The challenges. What she despises are the clients who insist there is a higher calling than the profit motive. CEOs are not renowned for reduced expectations.

Perhaps, she thought, she has, without realizing, tailored her expectations to living a life untethered to a sense of purpose, to marriage or family, residing, in effect, between the lines, within the white space of ambiguity.

The Rabbi's exhortation haunts her still. *What is the question to which your life in the answer?*

She wonders now if she will ultimately die without answering that terribly important question.

She recalled a conversation with Ruth when she was a child, after an uncle passed away unexpectedly.

What does it mean to die? she asked.

Everyone and everything dies, Ruth answered. *That's the natural way. They're not completely gone. They're in your heart, in your memory. You will hear their voices sometimes.*

After a lethargic unproductive weekend, Deana drove to work Monday morning listening for her mother's voice, but she heard nothing. After an early meeting, she closed her office door, with instructions to her assistant not to be disturbed, and called Simon Berman, director of administration at the cemetery who had scribbled his signature on the letter.

This is Shimon, he announced when he came on the line, with an unmistakable Israeli accent. Deana remembers how her mother used to say the Israelis are the exalted ones, the keepers of the flame, so to speak, although many are secular. Nevertheless, their diction, their commitment to a Jewish homeland, seems the personification of religious identity, as if a reproach to all others.

Although Deana grew up in a predominantly Jewish community and completed the childhood studies required to become a Bat Mitzvah, Judaism remains baffling. The more devout followers question and debate the meaning of just about everything on a seemingly endless quest for absolute truths, even as they profess such truths may not exist. Jason often said, even as he searched for empirical truths, the perpetual inquiry integral to Jewish life made certainty of anything except an omniscient God impossible. This seems to Deana the heart of Judaism: to paradoxically challenge and humble oneself to the faith. A profound ambiguity.

Is it no wonder she's ambivalent?

This is quite a turn of events, isn't it, Mrs. Rosner? the administrator responded when she introduced herself.

Ms, Deana corrected.

Ms. Yes, Ms. Rosner. Star of David Cemetery deeply regrets this situation.

Please explain to me the specifics of this situation. Seriously, how could this happen?

Yes, well, many caskets required storage that year. The ground was frozen unusually long, I'm told. I wasn't here then...

I know all that, Deana interrupted. *What I do not know is why my mother's casket was left there and not buried all this time!*

Your mother's casket was secured in the back-up vault and we had a different labeling system then, not as well defined, so it must have been assumed to be in rotation.

For ten years?

Yes, it is most unusual...

But how can you be sure it's my mother?

There is a casket code, like an SKU in a retail store. Technology does make some things easier.

He paused, as if they might casually converse about technology. Deana's silence was her response, so he continued.

Our new interment manager realized this casket may not have been moved for some time.

Some time? That's an understatement. And can you say for certain no one else was buried in my parents' plot?

Our database does not indicate this.

You will open the gravesite to be sure, yes?

An exhumation, yes, which is different from a dig, which requires authorization, from... Deana heard him shuffling papers. *Leo Rosner.*

Seriously? Deana roared. *Mr. Berman, this oversight, as you call it, may have extended to setting a stone over an empty plot, which is bad enough, or over another person, far worse, so don't you think you should take action right now? For God's sake, my mother was supposed to be buried ten years ago!*

And we will, but the cemetery cannot proceed without authorization from the conservator. In writing.

My brother lives in Europe.

We can email or fax the form. If he will sign, scan and return, we'll waive requirement for a notary.

How good of you, Deana snarled. *Email the form to Leo and send a form granting authority to me in his place. I'll be the primary contact from now on.*

Yes, well, all right, rather unusual, but, given the circumstances...

Mr. Berman. My brother and I want this travesty to be corrected at once, and I mean right now, so my mother may finally rest in peace.

Yes, Mrs., Ms. Rosner. Again, our condolences, he answered.

Again, Deana felt as if her mother had only just died. Worse than she felt ten years ago, because then it was a relief Ruth was no longer suffering.

After a long day on the job, Deana took the half-hour drive home on autopilot, as she often does. Usually she listens to radio news or a podcast. Today, staring listlessly ahead at the mass of brake lights, she was struck by a macabre image of her mother: alive and trapped inside the casket, screaming and scraping her nails against the sides, frantic to be free. Deana had to pull off the road to still her pounding heart.

Once at home, she lurched to a stop in the driveway and charged into the townhouse as if being chased by a goblin. She dropped her things in the hall and in the kitchen opened a bottle of red wine and left it on the counter to breathe. She dumped whatever she found in the salad bin into a large bowl – a bunch of arugula, shredded carrots, cherry tomatoes – and added olives from a jar in the refrigerator and a handful of candied walnuts. She drizzled in olive oil, lemon juice, balsamic vinegar and sea salt, and tossed, but in the end, she had no appetite. She put the salad aside and sipped the wine.

Her head hurt. All she wanted to do was dismiss this mess from her mind. She wanted to remember the best memories of her mother, of her parents, happily married for so many years. She did not want to think about them separated so long while Ruth was stuck in transition like Dickens' ghosts. Nevertheless, she had one more call to make, to the Rabbi, a favorite of her mother's who, she discovered earlier in the day, when she called the synagogue, had retired. Deana never knew him well. She was in college when he took over at the temple and her marriage had been officiated by Jason's recently ordained cousin.

Deana called him because they advised her that he made himself available to former congregants.

Oh, uh, Rabbi, she stuttered when he answered the phone, the sound of his voice rattling her as if he too had emerged from the grave. *You probably won't remember me; I'm Ruth Rosner's daughter, Deana. My mother...*

Of course I remember you, Deana, he answered. *I was a great fan of your mom, may she rest in peace. How are you?*

Thank you, Rabbi. I'm fine, thanks, well, mostly fine. I'm calling because, and this will sound quite strange, but my mother cannot rest in peace because she is not exactly at rest.

How do you mean, dear?

Once she explained, the Rabbi dismissed his practiced composure.

A travesty! Madness! How could this happen?

She explained the situation and said, *Rabbi, I mean no disrespect, please, but I have to ask, you were meant to go to the cemetery after the thaw, when the casket was interred. Do you remember doing that? I ask because we haven't yet ascertained if the plot is vacant or if another person was mistakenly buried there.*

Oy! I remember the service at the temple, of course, but in that weather I perform Kaddish at the cemetery after the fact. Often several in a day. Although sometimes the cemetery takes care of that.

That was ten years ago, hard to recall, I'm sure, and the cemetery cannot confirm one way or another. Would you have a record?

I'll check with the office tomorrow. But my dear, it's of no consequence. We must say the burial prayer and I would like to do that for you. For Ruth.

Deana sighed, relieved, by virtue of the Rabbi's attention, that her mother's life, and death, might be redeemed.

Thank you, Rabbi. That would mean so much to her. To all of us.

This must be terribly troubling for you, he said, with a kindness that shredded the last of her defenses.

I remember how devoted you were to your mother when she was ill. How gratifying it was for her to have you near. Your brother as well. How are you?

And your husband? I do hope you are finding your life to be meaningful. Should you wish to talk, I would be happy to see you. Once a Rebbe, always a Rebbe. My wife will attest to that. He chuckled.

Deana was struck dumb. She had to hold back from blathering all her misdeeds. Declaring her ambivalence toward just about everything and confessing she has yet to articulate the question to which her existence is the answer. She knew the Rabbi would be sympathetic. Such a man is forgiving, and she sorely needed to confess her sins, so to speak, to make sense of both past and future.

Nonetheless, she held her tongue. What would she tell him anyway? That she's a successful rational woman ruled by passion, with no real sense of purpose.

A woman who has spent her entire life trying not to be like her mother and so wishes now she were.

The cemetery called at the end of the day to report the gravesite was open, empty and properly prepared, and arrangements had been made for the Rabbi to preside over her mother's burial the following afternoon. Deana glanced at the calendar. Ruth would be buried in daylight and the first Hanukah candle lit at sunset.

Hanukkah commemorates the rededication of the temple at Jerusalem. *The rededication of freedom,* Ruth used to recite as she lit the Shamash, the candle designated to light all the others, adding another candle each night for eight nights. Ruth delighted as much in the word Hanukkah as the holiday, as it derives from the Hebrew verb meaning to dedicate.

Dedicate. Dedication to ideals, Deana muttered. *To the golden rule. To the people you love.*

The last time they celebrated together was when Ruth resided at Hospice. She was heavily medicated and had slipped in and out of sleep for days. That night, however, as if intuiting the holiday, she stayed awake. Deana presided over the ceremonial candle lighting, they all recited the prayer, and Leo led them in song. When Deana invited her mother to reach into a paper bag for a gift, Ruth, even in a weakened state, scolded her daughter.

Hanukkah is for the children, she groused.

Leo replied, *Mom, we're all someone's child.*

At these words, tears slipped from Ruth's eyes, likely recalling her own parents, whom, she had told Deana just that morning, she looked forward to seeing again soon. A precept Deana never realized existed in Jewish ideology, but which she thought must be a comfort to the faithful, like her mother.

Ruth, with obvious effort, reached into the bag to withdraw a bar of her favorite chocolate, eliciting a grateful smile. Her last smile. She slipped into a coma later that night and died the next day.

After the mortuary claimed the body, Deana gathered the last of her mother's belongings, and when she discovered the unopened chocolate bar on the bedside table, she was overcome with grief. She never imagined she could feel as sad as she felt that day, even more than the day her father died, until the day Jason moved out, and then, all these years later, the day she received the letter from the cemetery.

The next evening, after sunset, as a thick cloud cover blanketed the moon, Deana lit Hanukkah candles and watched them burn, mesmerized by the tiny flames, a stream of blue light rising as if lighting the way to liberation.

Afterward, she dined on crispy potato latkes smothered in applesauce, the way her mother served them, and then, with a glass of sweet wine in hand, she sent a confirmation email to Leo. The crisis was over.

He called the next morning. *There's certain symmetry here, don't you think?*

Hanukkah you mean?

Yes. Seems like yesterday.

Deana nodded, as if Leo could see. *I realize this mess was just an insane and inexplicable error, but I feel I failed her.*

We didn't fail her, we saved her. YOU saved her. And D, you should go to the cemetery. Once the stone is reset.

Why?

Because, if you're there, she'll know she's in the right place.

And you think only if I stand there, she will know?

I think, if you stand there, YOU will know. And then you both might rest in peace.

A Good Enough Woman

By day, you write marketing materials and churn out press releases, waging battle on behalf of your clients with the aggression of a mountain lion. By night, you write stories no one reads. Stories about women traveling the globe in search of significance, women chasing romance, women avoiding intimacy or longing for what they might have had but never had the courage to reach for, also tales of men trying to make sense of their own existence, and their women.

None of the stories are quite right, not one, after all these years, as many as eighty or ninety, more to come, stored on flash drives or the Cloud, otherwise invisible. Indefensible.

Besides, there has never been much time between the public relations projects, Pilates classes, supermarketing and school pickups, trips to the shoemaker, the dry cleaner or the farmer's market – all the errands you run when your daughters are at dance class or soccer, play rehearsal or study group or, over time, hanging with friends at the library, the park or the teen center, ogling adolescent boys, whispering secrets with gal pals, hopefully harmless gossip, because the dark secrets are a mother's nightmare.

When daily obligations have been met, the little time to spare, the stolen hours, you think of them, when most women share confidences over coffee or buy pretty things, you head to the bookstore.

The proprietor is a woman patrons and staff refer to affectionately and reverently as the Diva. A tall white-haired woman with sparkling eyes and wit, she presides over the shop with the precision of a librarian, which she was when younger. She has the grace of a stage actress and the memory of an elephant – she recognizes her customers by name, she remembers their children and grandchildren, their interests and pastimes, and what types of books they prefer. She wears red, every day, every shade of red from apple to claret, her favorite color, also the personification of the red wagon store logo. One large red candle burns from opening to closing, behind the register, its smoke lilting a sweet apple and cinnamon fragrance as if pie in the oven, and a scaled-down genuine red flyer sits in the display window, overflowing with the Diva's favorite titles of the season, which you check each time you arrive to be sure you are current.

The Diva pays you generously for the hours you can spare. She treasures your literary persona. At the bookstore you are not a mountain lion or a mother lion, not a housekeeper, wife or discouraged writer. There you guide customers through the labyrinth of new fiction and personal favorites from the backlist and, what you most enjoy, recommend titles for reading groups. You suggest themes or overlooked novels that should be revisited. Story anthologies for readers tight for time and poetry for the romantics. For highbrow bookworms, you pair classics with post-modern fiction. Avid readers are avid shoppers and you are happy to help them make the most of their selections, although you have never joined a book group because even one book, one more obligation, would be just another chore that interferes with your writing time.

At the bookstore, the many writers you admire seduce you as if lovers. Serious writers who teach you and taunt you. They call to you from the shelves, like the pile of books on the nightstand calls to you. Nevertheless, this break in the day at the bookstore is the best time of day, moments that come and go as quickly as a sudden summer storm, after which you can breathe more easily fresher air.

Late evening is the one time you call your own. After dinner dishes washed, laundry folded while still warm, emails answered and archived and the final touches placed on client work, and after the daily daughter drama is mitigated, after your girls are safely tucked in for the night, although, over time, they refuse tucking, they barely tolerate a kiss on the forehead or a hug and roll their eyes at the very idea of a recitation of pages from one of the classics you insisted on reading to them when they were younger. That used to be your favorite time of day. Too soon they began reading to themselves or burying their eyes and ears in music or videos, doors closed, their adolescence shrouded in the mystery you were not permitted at that age.

It is then you retreat to the bedroom, deserted most weeknights, because your husband's business often takes him to European and Asian capitals, places you long to see, but someone has to be home. He is always on the job, he says, enduring long days of meetings and dinners, sometimes at Michelin-rated restaurants or after-dinner drinks at hotel bars and, if he stays the weekend, engaging clients on a golf course. He tells you there is little time to fully experience these legendary cities. At best, a glimpse of the countryside from a train, a quick guided tour, a meander through an old quarter. You would be bored, he says.

You love trains – the clack on the tracks, the scent of past lives and the pulse of momentum. You dream of taking the high-speed train from Brussels to Berlin, Madrid to Barcelona. You would like to ride the Orient Express through the rugged Russian terrain or the new Janakpur Railway through Nepal. You suspect, however, by the time your daughters are grown and you make time for such adventures, your husband will have grown tired of planes, trains and foreign language, and you will not travel far.

When he is at home, you spend evenings in the den watching one or another old or new film on a large television screen, the so-called Smart TV. Most often you read while he watches; he requires only proximity. When you were first married, you lamented every departure and every lonely night. Now you favor solitude, not because your husband is demanding, he is not, just one less thing to attend to.

On the nights you are on your own, you go directly to your bedroom and carve out your space in the center of the king bed. The walls are champagne neutral, bedding and draperies with dark green accents. Large oak chests line one wall and matching narrow side tables flank the bed, their tops chiseled in copper. You toss the floral decorative cushions from the bed to a rarely used chaise in the corner and plump up three of the four sleeping pillows for elevation, leaving the fourth to bolster the laptop. You neatly fold a billowy comforter halfway down the bed to pull up over your body later in the night. Space prepared, you cleanse and moisturize your face, brush and floss your teeth, massage a blob of cream into your hands and smooth the residue up your neck, and then slip out of your clothes and put on oversized boxer shorts and one of the T-shirts you sleep in, T-shirts too old and faded to wear during the day, but soft and comfy at night. The room is lit only by the glow of the laptop. You write, you edit, you hunt for words stuck in your brain and inventive metaphors or eccentric character traits. Too soon your eyes grow tired. You never last long. You succumb to sleep as if a trance, cradled by all three cushy pillows, hardly a moment to take stock of the day or the writing. You sleep soundly for four or five hours before you wake, roughly the same time every night, well into the night, but well before dawn. The bedroom, the house, the neighborhood, all eerily, divinely silent, stillness parsed only by the subtle ticking of a hall clock.

Now is your time to read. Magnifiers wait on the nightstand with a pitcher of water. A bedside lamp illuminates pages like the flashlight you used when you were a girl, when you were also supposed to be sleeping.

While you read, you have the profoundly dispirited conviction there are so many superb writers, so many original stories, there is no need for more. You will never be as good, so what is the point? On the other hand, there are museums throughout the world filled with exquisite paintings and sculptures yet, just the other day, you admired a watercolor in a gallery window near the bookstore. There is always room for more, you hope, so the next day, when the darkness settles in and the house is still, you return to the writing, because this is all you have ever wanted to do. You mean only to be far better than you are.

A good enough writer is never good enough. A good enough mother has to be.

You learned this when your elder daughter turned twelve. Overnight, it seemed, she transformed from a sweet, sensitive girl, a little anxious, tentative, into a moody, sullen, raging adolescent. You were ill-equipped for the brutality of her distemper and you so much wanted to ease her distress, also diminish the daily door slams and the venomous rhetoric that made you weep into your pillow and your husband bury himself in escapist fiction, and your younger daughter withdraw deeper into her protective shell.

You attended a PTA meeting where a family therapist discusses the writings of D.W. Winnicott, a pediatrician and psychoanalyst who posited the often-cited theory of the good enough mother.

The next morning, you were at the library the moment the doors opened, where you dropped onto the worn carpet right there in the stacks to peruse his landmark book, *Playing and Reality.* Leaning against metal shelving with your legs crossed like a yogi, you read for three hours until your back ached and the concept began to sink in, and then you ordered a copy from the bookstore, which you read oh so carefully, a pen in hand to underline key points. There were many.

The good enough mother acknowledges and accepts her flaws, and reveals them to the child in order to minimize the inevitable disappointment derived from artificial expectations. This makes perfect sense. You know dissatisfaction is the result of improbable ideals. You saw that in your own mother, didn't you? A life tethered to obligation and to the illusions engraved in the archetypes of a patriarchal culture. A good enough mother helps children understand that parents are neither omnipotent nor perfect and, in turn, we must accept each child as is – not a mirror image, nor a manifestation of missed opportunities. All easier said than done, you think, but you hang on every word.

When you pick up your daughters at school that day, overflowing with good intentions, your firstborn announces she should never have been born to you. She says you don't understand her and you never will and she cannot wait to get out of your house.

You would never have spoken to your parents this way – nothing less than blanket acceptance of the rules, no matter how arbitrary they seemed, and gratitude for the hard work and sacrifices made so that your life would be a better life. The mere hint of adversarial body language or a remark perceived to be acrimonious or disrespectful and you would have been punished with additional chores and grounding. Your father might have raised his hand to you. You would have been made to feel small, an ingrate, as many of us were made to feel, so when angry thoughts came to mind, you sealed your lips. You were ashamed. You believed you were not a good enough daughter and now you are not a good enough mother.

You meet with the therapist who spoke at the PTA gathering. She is cordial and direct, and she knows what you feel. Of course she understands – did you believe you were better because you wanted to be better? Did you think other mothers know more than you or have superior skills? Most mothers are good enough and most women are better than they believe themselves to be.

You tearfully explain to your husband about good enough parenting. He's not sure what to make of the state you're in. You are so steady, as a rule. So rational. He relies on your reliability. He wants what's best for you and his children, but this conflict has caught him off guard and he wants peace restored to the house where he comes home to rest.

You tell him you want to sign on with the therapist. A short time, a few months, you say, might teach you technique and insight and ease the tension. Three years later, you have learned more about yourself than you could have invented for a hundred stories.

You find yourself reconsidering your mother and your grandmother, whose voices you hear often in your head. You understand better now that we all do the best we can, an expression you heard me say many times. No mother is perfect, no woman is perfect, no human is perfect, but few are truly terrible. Most of us have the best of intentions. Most of us are good enough. Do you see that now?

A good enough mother makes sense. A good enough woman is the best you can be. A good enough writer? No, you fear. Never good enough.

Children mature, husbands slow down, lives simplify. Peace is restored at home as your girls find their way. You see the signs of maturity on your body. Parents age and pass on. Friends retire. They battle disease. You do all you can for them. Your husband pays the last college tuition bill. He says you can work less now because the retirement fund is on track and the expense of an empty nest far less. At last, you think, you will devote more time to writing.

The morning you feel the lump in your breast, you know time has run out. Hard and amorphous like a pebble and deep enough to have hidden for too long, screaming now for discovery. You too would scream if you were the sort of woman to scream. If not for the torrential shower, you would hear me scream for you.

How can this be? You responsibly and regularly performed self-examinations in the shower or prone on the bed, gently pressing each breast with your palm in a circular motion.

Your heart beats wildly as you press again on the breast, as if whatever you felt might have disappeared, like a cyst or an inflammation that retracts in the heat, but it is still there. Of course it is. You knew what you felt the moment you felt it, you have been taught to feel for it, to fear it, and you know at once what will come next.

You are one of the four now.

You stand in the stall as still as a mannequin, body cleansed, hair shampooed and conditioned, legs shaved, hot water beating down on your shoulders and dripping down your pendulous breasts, breasts the source of sexual arousal and the source of nourishment for your babies. They hang lower now, flatter and fleshy, fondled less often, admired rarely, and likely headed for annihilation.

You dress unusually slowly that morning. You do not bother to make your bed or wash the breakfast dishes. No one will notice. You forget to apply makeup and perfunctorily brush your hair. You drive directly to the bookstore and stay until closing, hiding like a reed within the marsh of book talk. The Diva comments that you seem pale and you say you are a little tired. She is not convinced. All the reading of so many books for so many years, she detects a story without words.

You don't tell anyone. Your daughters both work in the city by the Bay, far enough but not too far. They live with roommates and have jobs sufficient to cover exorbitant rents, with help from parents. Your husband has taken a new project in Maryland, where he expects to spend a week a month, maybe more, for a year or so. He assures you no longer than that. As much as he says he would like to retire, he is pleased by this endorsement for his expertise.

Just one more, he promises.

You tell him you too have a prospective client, in Los Angeles, and must go there to seal the deal. He does not question the commitment. No reason to.

You have made an appointment to see an oncologist at a prestigious medical center. You claimed to have no insurance and will pay the fee at the time of the visit. Before you make the trip, you open a bank account online. You set up paperless communications with secret ID's and passwords. You pay for the visit with the new debit card, so your husband cannot trace the bill.

The nurse inquires when you had your last mammogram and you say you are perhaps six months overdue. You lost track of time, you confess, although you had little cause for concern, despite your grandmother's history. After all, you are only fifty-four years old. You exercise and eat well and you nursed two babies for a year. The doctor refers you for a diagnostic mammogram and you can tell from the expression in the technician's eyes your prognosis may be worse than even a self-diagnosis suggests. When the doctor calls with next steps, you tell him your family is in the midst of moving out of state and you will seek treatment there through your new insurance.

The nurse sends a digital copy of your scan in preparation for a biopsy. You are in a funky café in Santa Monica when the file lands in your phone's inbox and you cannot keep from glancing at the ugly image before you hide the mail in a miscellaneous folder. You take only a few bites of beetroot hummus with toasted flatbread that sounded delicious when you ordered. The waitress asks if everything is all right with the food. *I guess my eyes are bigger than my stomach,* you say. She wraps the remains in a box which you chuck into a dumpster in the parking lot.

You will not seek treatment. You have wasted enough time and you will not put your children or husband through this. They have lives to live, as do you, whatever life is left.

A few hours into the drive north, you stop to wander a small town along the water that you once read about in a travel blog and where you find a sweet rental cottage on a quiet street in walking distance to an untrammeled stretch of beach. In that moment, you plan your escape with the same meticulous attention to detail you have given to work, home and family. You tell the landlord you are taking a writer's retreat and you pay six months rent in advance. You tell your husband and daughters and friends the same. The girls applaud your resolve and your friends admire your independence.

Your husband says he's proud of you. When you pack, and he realizes you're really leaving, he says he wishes he could come with you.

Although, he pronounces with pride, *this venture should complete the retirement fund.*

He does not know he will retire on his own and you are ashamed of your deception, but plans have been made. No turning back. He proposes weekend visits and you answer that you hope to immerse yourself in the writing 24/7. He is baffled by your detachment. He wonders if there is anything else he should know and you assure him you are merely taking a huge step toward a lifelong goal, but you will of course make time for visits.

Your daughters suggest to their father you may be suffering a late mid-life crisis. Might be menopausal madness, they say. They chuckle about it.

You take the barest of necessities: a thesaurus and laptop, a bundle of journals. A Kindle loaded with samples to decide later your reading list. You pack the coffee mug one of your daughters made for you when she was in elementary school, with their smiling childhood faces on it. A well-worn robe, cozy sleeping clothes, slouchy day clothes and good walking shoes. You wear your wedding band and a carved silver ring bequeathed from your grandmother to your mother and then to you, and a sapphire pendant necklace your husband gave you on your 50th birthday. You leave all else behind and discover how little you need to be you.

The cottage is furnished in shades of sand and sea – jute rugs under rattan chairs, a sofa covered in azure sailcloth with tan throw pillows, bedding in sky blue stripes and a quilt adorned with drawings of clamshells. The place is overflowing with the essentials for an extended stay, from beach towels to bicycles, a wine cooler, picnic basket, sand chairs, and a large shade umbrella. Perfect for long writing days and strolls along the shoreline and perhaps, during the warmer months, a squat on the beach.

You settle in quickly. From day one, you rise at dawn to saunter along tree-lined streets into town. It is early spring. You bundle up with a fleece jacket and scarf against the morning sea breezes. Off-season is tranquil; in summer, you're told, the town will blast like a beehive under assault. You move quickly enough to stretch your legs and generate heat under your skin, but slowly enough to observe your new surroundings. The village might serve well as the setting for a story and you take an inventory of landmarks: the obligatory

19th century church, a tiny harbor, the clang of masts echoing the wind, and a community center where a schoolhouse once stood, incorporating a museum of local maritime history.

Along Main Street, residents acknowledge each other by name. They share breakfasts at cafés where the cooks know their tastes and where they commiserate over erratic weather and better times in another time. They glance up and smile when you enter and call to you to have a good day when you leave. Their pick-up trucks are lined up in tidy rows like the vegetables on nearby farmland.

Next door to your cottage, two middle-aged men reside in a bungalow surrounded by dense bushes of star jasmine and lavender. A sugary fragrance fills the air. Both are dark-haired and burly and have thick facial hair, as if they have been on a long journey. Friendly grins burst from their nests. The younger of the two waves to you as you return from your morning walk and you stop for introductions. He says they moved there from Colorado five years ago and spend a few months a year in a famous colonial city in Mexico where they plan to retire. They work from home – the younger organizes tours to Latin America, the older is a software developer. He invites you to dinner.

You notice a tile by their front door inscribed, *please remove your shoes*, so you go into town for a pedicure. You haven't had one in years. A young Asian woman, Thai or Vietnamese, leans down to your feet to scrape away dry skin and trim cuticles. She is very thin, her hair is nearly black and straight to the shoulder like string, and she never smiles. When she massages warm body oil onto your legs, pressing in hypnotically slow pressure from knees to toes and deep into the soles of your feet, you lay your head back and close your eyes and relax in a way you haven't relaxed in longer than you can remember. After your toenails are tinted the deep purple you chose from a line-up of tiny jars by the front door, she pats your hand and suggests you sit until the polish dries. She sets a timer.

You stare at your feet as if they belong to someone else. You imagine a short story about a young woman who polishes hundreds of toenails every day for a lifetime. What might have happened to her to bring her to this place and what might have to happen to alter her destiny?

You arrive for dinner that night with a green salad brimming with slivers of red onion and split cherry tomatoes, topped with lumps of goat cheese, and with a bottle of wine from the Santa Ynez Valley recommended by the local wine shop.

A large bowl of guacamole, an avocado pit in the center, waits on a coffee table between two short couches – you sit on one, they face you from the other. They pour red wine sangria from a pitcher filled with chunks of fruit into bulbous glasses with cobalt blue trim. You scoop the guacamole eagerly with triangular corn chips that have been warmed in the oven. Salt and lime and cilantro delight the taste buds.

Their home is accessorized with Mexican folk art. A skull on the fireplace mantle, carved like a jack-o-lantern, is a relic of a Day of the Dead celebration. *Dio de los Muertos*, the younger neighbor explains. A discussion ensues about ghosts and ghouls versus spirits and the transmigration of souls. You would like to believe you will return, although you have never thought much about it. They say they hope to resurrect as owls or whales, wise and formidable, and they laugh heartily at such fanciful notions.

The older and larger of the couple, the better chef, he claims, grills a slab of salmon to serve with the salad. He squeezes lemon generously over the fish and the citrus scent is tantalizing. The younger uncorks the white wine and invites you to the table. For two hours, you all share your life stories, and when they ask about your writing, you answer no, you are not yet published and you are working on a story collection, but you fail to mention you have been working on that collection for more than twenty years.

You don't remember the last time you were at an intimate getting acquainted dinner. These neighbors are easy to be with. They gush over good food and wine, they look forward to fulfilling their modest aspirations. You welcome this rare gift of new friends and enjoy the exalted persona of the writer, although you are not yet writing.

You go to sleep early and sleep through the night, perhaps compensation for too many years of restlessness.

The next weekend, you invite your neighbors for afternoon tea and they bring brownies laced with marijuana. Between the chocolate chips are tiny bits of green, like the remains of freshly mown grass, and the brownies taste loamy. Laughter reverberates through the cottage all afternoon and you sleep even more soundly through the night. You save the leftovers in the freezer for the pain that is sure to come, although you have never felt better. As if the crevices within your body have been filled with fresh mortar.

You savor the pretense you have created and on your next morning walk, you contemplate a story about a woman with cancer who cheats death. The woman in this story might have a miraculous recovery. Would that be believable?

You download books of great writers you have been meaning to read or re-read – D.H. Lawrence, Faulkner, Kafka, Bellow, Tessa Hadley and A.S. Byatt. The Diva has sent you off with a pile of paperback story anthologies and each morning, after your walk, you read one with the second mug of coffee you prepare in the machine you previously disdained as offensive to the environment, but which makes you inexplicably happy every time you pop in a single serve coffee pod and within seconds have a steaming fresh brew.

Your husband grows impatient. You have been gone nearly a month without a visit and he jokes that you must be shacking up with another man. You assure him the only men in your life are the gay men next door and you are writing or reading around the clock.

He invites you to Washington, DC for the weekend to celebrate your birthday. Another year must be honored, never more so than this year. *Double digits*, he exclaims, as if a prize. You fly to New York first to spend time with an old friend. You wander the Met for hours and linger over dinner discussing politics and culture and what ails modern generations, as old friends do, without revealing your condition. Why ruin a lovely visit?

In the morning, you board the train, relishing the steady forward motion and the quiet so much you're almost sorry to arrive.

With your husband, you visit the Martin Luther King memorial, wisdom engraved into marble for posterity, and you linger a long time at the Korean War commemoration, mesmerized by the eerie ashen life-sized specters of death that nevertheless radiate life. In the glow of the reflecting pool, you are inspired by so many so far beyond good enough.

You enjoy birthday dinner at a hip restaurant housed in a historic inn.

Today you are fifty-five years old, not a prime number, but a multiple of prime numbers. Must be auspicious, your husband says.

You toast another year with champagne. He is happy to be with you. He is usually the one to leave; now he has been left behind and he's gone to great lengths to please. A meal of six small plates sates your appetite and waiters croon happy birthday presenting a thick slice of chocolate mousse cake with one candle lit. As you blow out the candle, your only wish is for your daughters' good health.

You sleep together at a fancy hotel near DuPont Circle, on an oversized pillow-top bed with a padded headboard. You both praise the high thread-count sheets and fluffy quilt.

In the privacy of your hotel room, city lights beyond your window, your husband caresses your breasts and licks your nipples, failing to notice the lump, as it is still largely buried like a jack-in-the-box yet to pop. He would have to press down on the breast to feel the interloper and he has always been a tender lover. When he abandons your breasts to put his lips to the soft flesh between your thighs, and then slips his tongue into the delicate crevices, tears stream down your cheeks even as you cry out with pleasure. He pulls you to him and presses himself deep within, deeper than usual, as if searching for you.

So it is true, he comments afterward, drowsy and content. *Absence makes the heart grow fonder.*

You might have countered that he has long been absent, but you do not, and later that night, at that hour when you usually wake to read, you turn toward your husband, wrap one arm over his chest and press your breasts to his back. Still sleeping, he takes your hand in his and you weep, silently. You've missed him all these years and you should tell him the truth. He would hold you and promise to make it better, but he cannot and you will not.

When the weekend ends, you promise another visit soon and then return to your cozy cottage to sleep alone again.

A few weeks later, when your daughters ask to visit, you tell them there is not much to do in the sleepy town. In truth, you do not wish to share this special place you've made your own, so you suggest you meet in Carmel. You book a suite at a bed and breakfast and when they arrive, enjoy lunch at a popular café before exploring the mission. Together you stroll down Ocean Avenue, stopping to peruse art gallery windows before landing at Carmel Beach to watch the sun set over the Pacific Ocean. The day is unexpectedly exhausting, so you dispatch your daughters to dine on their own and turn in early, and when they return, staying up late to watch a movie, you listen from your bed, cherishing their intimate voices and laughter, until you can no longer stay awake. The next day, you all hike the rocky Point Lobos reserve, delighting in glimpses of sea otters and seals along the shoreline, and after dinner on a rooftop, sweetened by sea breezes and smiles, you sleep – fresh air, a long walk and the pleasure of your daughters' company salves to your wounds.

Your older daughter says she does not remember ever seeing you so mellow. The younger says you seem to have found a new center. They attribute this to the devotion to the writing and they say they're happy for you. You are pained by the subterfuge, but pleased they think of you this way. You would like to be remembered as such. When time to leave, you hug them close, as if babies again, reluctant to let go.

You should have told them the truth. They deserve to hear this from you, but you could not bring yourself to ruin a precious visit. Could this be the last visit? An unbearable thought.

When you return to the cottage, the older neighbor stops to chat and he asks if you're feeling well.

You seem a bit wan, he says.

You tell him you walked too much and stayed up too late with your daughters.

I just need to catch up on sleep. I could use more of those brownies, you say, and he obliges.

You cut them into bite size portions and freeze for future medicinal use.

You have been told a tumor doesn't hurt, but before long you ache, a pain deep under your ribs, and your clavicle feels like it might snap like a twig in a stiff wind. You take the train to Union Station, Los Angeles, and walk to Chinatown to purchase herbal painkillers and teas. You follow the sound of celebratory music to the Ghost Festival at the Thien Hau Temple, which welcomes the spirits of ancestors. It is said that ghosts return this day each year, from both the upper and lower realms, to mingle and seek redemption, and you close your eyes and imagine your own ancestors, all of us also just good enough, and think about how your daughters will imagine you when you're gone, although you dismiss the notion of the end of your life. Not yet.

On the train ride back to your cloistered life, comforted by the steady rumbling and the vast blue of ocean and sky, you murmur a prayer not for salvation or miracles, but courage.

The tumor grows. A section of your breast is red and itchy now and the skin begins to swell and crack like a dry riverbed. You purchase lightweight oversized T-shirts that won't rub against your skin in the late summer heat. You try to sleep on your back, although each time you turn over you awaken in pain, so you put a pillow over your midline to keep you in place, as you did in the late months of pregnancy. You are overwhelmed with melancholy, longing for the joyfulness that comes with anticipation – the making of a life instead of the waning.

You know you've been foolish. A woman with means and good health has a greater chance of survival. Still, your decision has brought you to a lovely place:

this place of tranquility and solitude that sustains your spirit, every day, despite the pain and despite regret.

Every morning, still in night clothes, you wrap yourself in a blanket and burrow into an Adirondack chair along the side of the house, facing east, sipping coffee as you watch the sun rise. For the first time in your life, you welcome the day more than the night.

You print out all the stories you've ever written on three-hole punched paper at the local print shop and gather the pages into large black binders, the sort of binders you used when you were a schoolgirl. Thousand of pages representing thousands of hours, over a hundred stories now, and although none are fully polished and none are perfect, they are not incomplete. In the aggregate, they are a life's work worth some satisfaction.

You are certain now you are where you were meant to be. You will enjoy every morning and every evening, and the hours between, as long as you're able, and you will face death with dignity, leaving behind artfully composed apologies for your daughters.

And that will have to be good enough.

The Sculptor

The child cries out, and Janet, half-asleep, dashes down the hall to the nursery before the next cry. The second round will be louder, escalating in waves to deafening – the pattern three months now, night after night, like a protracted hurricane. The night terrors, they are called, and they are, for mother and child.

Ron murmurs as she rises from bed, *I'll go.*

Sleep, Janet whispers, the usual response, because she takes her maternal responsibility seriously and because her husband is up at dawn to face the drive to work. He made partner at the law firm shortly before Melanie was born, as planned, yet still works long hours. Janet works half–time now, at the Museum of Contemporary Art. She had achieved the position of membership director and then, following an extended maternity leave, negotiated reduced hours: on-site Tuesdays, Thursdays, and in attendance at major staff meetings, the balance of time from home. It is only fair, she believes, she should deal with the nightly wake-up call. More to the point, she is certain these terrors have something to do with her.

Melanie stands in her crib, clutching the railing like a prisoner condemned to serving time for a crime she did not commit. She is small for her age, petite, like

Janet, thus all the more defenseless. Large dark brown eyes stare blankly at the window. Her lips quiver. The pediatrician described this state as hallucinatory, not a dream and not a nightmare. A primal terror with no detectable cause or correlation, he explained.

Janet would like to believe him, but she is certain there is always a cause, always a correlation, and if not a solution, a resolution. Ron agrees, in principle, although he has accepted his naiveté as a father.

It's all right, Janet coos to the child.

She has been instructed not to touch her, not to startle her. She counts to sixty, slowly, silently, before leaning in to pat Melanie's upper back and then gently ruffle her dark wavy hair, hair that came in late but filled in so quickly and so thick, she seems an incarnate of Medusa. Ringlets fan her head like the mythological snakes, reminding Janet of Caravaggio's painting of the gorgon, whose power, according to Greek legend, was to turn those who might gaze on her to stone. That image these days sends shivers down her spine.

Melanie might have been born of the sea, conceived on their third anniversary holiday to Bonaire, a Caribbean coral reef a short distance from Venezuela. Mornings, and most afternoons, Janet and Ron donned scuba diving gear and descended into crystal-clear warm water to explore spiny sea urchins and tiny frogfish the colors of the rainbow. Janet delighted in the underwater hush, punctuated only by the muffled ebb and flow of her breathing. She had not experienced such serenity since her rare free time at college, when she sat for hours at a sculptor's table, her breath echoed by the chisel, a steady determined chipping as soothing as the surf. After the last dive of the day, they retired to their room, showered off salt and sand, and made love to the hum of a ceiling fan. They napped until dinner, lulled by the heat and the inner sway of the sea. It was on one of those languorous afternoons when Janet felt something like bubbles rising from her pelvis, as if from the depths of the underworld, and she imagined her child a mermaid, bright as sunlight on a turquoise sea, although these nights, murky and mysterious.

Sleep little love, Janet whispers. *You're safe. Mama is here.* A nightly mantra she devised on the recommendation of a sleep coach she discovered in an ad on the back page of a parenting magazine.

What a way to make a living, Ron snickered at the time.

A specialty for everything, Janet answered, grateful for the expertise and the hope that came with it.

She followed the coach's instructions and reported daily on progress, rather the lack of progress. After nine weeks, the coach confessed she too was baffled, such things passing in days or weeks, as a rule.

Melanie's cries dwindle to shudders before her body grows slack and she crumples to the mattress. The first flight has passed. Janet stays in place awaiting the next round. She tenderly rubs her daughter's back. *Shhhh,* she murmurs, like an island wind. Melanie folds her arms under her belly, butt elevated, flushed cheek pressed to the sheet. The pose of innocence. Virtue. Janet has the thought that Michelangelo might have signed that figure to place with the Pieta.

Medical experts cautioned against newborns sleeping on the chest to prevent choking or suffocation. Janet was vigilant on this, of course, but by seven months old, Melanie could flip over and right herself, and turn her head side to side, proving her ability to remove herself from harm's way, so she was permitted to sleep on her belly and, at last slept through the night.

After five nights of unbroken sleep, the parents celebrated.

Here's to the end of sleep deprivation, Ron toasted with champagne.

They lingered over lovemaking like newlyweds. They rose each morning with the light, their energy levels improved and they all settled into a predictable routine. Nine months later, as if a rebirth, the terrors began, and Janet was reminded, as she has been repeatedly since the birth, nothing is foreseeable now. No matter the organization, the coaches and doctors and parenting literature, each day an amorphous mound of clay.

Melanie breathes evenly. Her torso gently rises and retracts with each breath. Janet slithers to the floor to recline on a pale gray carpet rimmed with stripes of terra cotta and aqua blue, a color scheme designed to be gender neutral. This was the first room she decorated in their first house. Curated, in effect. She painted the walls pale coral to set off the white furniture and hung billowy sheer white curtains, like an island villa.

Janet curls into a fetal position on the rug, pulling a decorative throw pillow off the antique chair where she had contentedly nursed and rocked her daughter to sleep when everything seemed on track. She feels herself slide into the sublime state of limbo that precedes sleep – behind her eyes, a midnight-blue sky filled with stars. And then, like a meteorite bursting into that sky, Melanie cries out again, this time a shriek so fierce Janet feels the fear as if her own. Sobs escalate to a frantic wail and Melanie strains to catch her breath, heaving so hard her tiny body shakes until, as if a demonic force has released its grip, she collapses and resettles into a resting pose.

Janet stays as still as a statue until the child sleeps and then stumbles down the hall and slips under the bedcovers, snuggling close to Ron for warmth.

The second round is the worst, she told the pediatrician last week at the 18-month check-up. *Sends chills up my spine. How can a child so young, so well loved, be wracked with terror? She eats well, she naps well. She wakes with a smile. By day, she's cheerful and friendly, so much so I fear she might walk off with any stranger who takes her hand.*

Melanie was sitting on Janet's lap, cheerfully twisting the doctor's stethoscope cord.

He nodded knowingly. *Anything new on the home front? Unusual stress?*

No. No change, no stress. We were settled into a routine. We were even talking about having another child.

Janet and Ron agreed from the first on two children. Siblings who might lean on each other and each get adequate attention from their parents. Even though easier with just one, Janet presumed she would rise to the challenge of parenting with her usual flair. Although juggling motherhood and career, she had no doubt she would strike a balance. She's a lifelong workhorse. At fourteen she was bagging groceries and paid her way through college with a combination of jobs she managed masterfully enough to graduate cum laude. She had planned to return to the museum after maternity leave, but she was besotted with her daughter, Ron's word, and wanted to be home with her more often than not. Good in theory; however in practice, daunting, and some days, and nights, Herculean.

The pediatrician observed Melanie closely while peeking into ears and eyes, tapping at pulse points and joints, searching for triggers a physician of nearly forty years would recognize.

Word count? Phrases? he asked.

At least fifty words. I've written most of them down. The first was cat, which she shouted incessantly for a while, but with a hard-g, gat, even though we don't have a cat. Fruits and berries. Animal names and sounds. Even names of books, well, her version of the names. She says please and thank you, and bless you, if you sneeze, and the other day, I pointed to a bee on a lavender bush and told her we never touch a bee, and she watched the bee very closely, as if she might figure the insect out, and then, a few days later, when we saw a bee, she said, no touch.

The pediatrician smiled. *Smart girl.*

I assumed by now she might string words together into longer sentences.

The baby tweeter, he said with a chuckle.

He concluded inscribing notes onto a laptop before he extricated his stethoscope from Melanie and turned his attention to Janet.

Babies come with emotional DNA, as unique as every other facet of their genome. We think we see and feel what they see and feel, but we don't. It's frankly impossible to comprehend what's prowling the recesses of their brains or what might upset the nervous system. They keep their secrets close. She won't remember any of it. This too shall pass.

Janet's mother also favored that platitude and Janet believes, deep down, it's true, although she's no longer certain of anything. Surely some things never pass; instead, they hide. They fester. They wreck a life.

She's doing fine, he reiterated. *And so are you.*

Janet nearly burst into tears, immensely grateful for the approbation she has not realized she desperately needs since the terrors began.

On her way to work the next morning, Janet drops Melanie at the home of Mrs. Angelos, a retired kindergarten teacher who watches over the girl for the extra dollars in her fixed-income pocket, and because her own grandchildren live far away. Short and round, with mocha skin and silver hair, she emanates kindness and good cheer, so much so that at the first interview, Melanie leapt from Janet's arms into Mrs. Angelos' lap, playing with her beaded necklace and burrowing into her body as if returning to the source.

Janet asked at the first interview, *do you have a particular parenting style? An approach that served well in the classroom?*

Every child is different. I listen to their hearts,
Mrs. Angelos answered. *I offer you only this advice,* she
said, recognizing a new mother's anxiety.

Please, Janet pleaded, because she never seeks
advice from her sister, who takes a radically different
approach to everything, or her mother, enjoying
retirement on the golf course and other than gifts and
regular visits, seems relieved to be free of obligation.

Kids change, Mrs. Angelos said. *Always the new,
also new joy, although at times, hard, like the
adolescents.* She chuckled. *Repeat, please, after me...
nothing is forever, all things are only now.*

All day Janet repeated those words, in the same
way she once memorized poetry. *Nothing is forever, all
things are only now.*

As much as she appreciated the optimism in the
sentiment, the now, these days, feels crushingly endless.

What Janet failed to mention to the pediatrician
or the babysitter, or her husband, is the panic she
experiences during the night terrors, because as
Melanie wails she turns unrecognizable, ugly, like a
creature in a fairy tale under the spell of a witch. Janet
has considered pressing a pillow over the child's face to
still the evil spirit. Perhaps the shock might bring her
sweet baby back to her. The thought makes her sick
with shame, however to do nothing, to simply accept
or wait something out that requires intervention, has
never been, for Janet, a rational course of action.

Melanie mutters odd words during the terrors,
as if in a trance. Sounds staccato and indecipherable.
Sometimes she growls like a feral animal. Janet would
call them nonsense if they were not uttered with the

194

ardor of an orator. She is convinced her daughter is trying to communicate something Janet needs to know, but she cannot fathom what she's saying, much less respond, and she fears an abyss has already formed between mother and daughter they might never cross.

Increasingly anxious, Janet gathers her courage to reach out to her mother to ask if she or her sister experienced anything like the terrors.

Not that I recall. I always hated when you girls cried but babies cry, you know. That's just what they do sometimes.

Not like this, Mom.

Hmmm… but you're so smart, Jan, you'll sort it out, her mother said, simultaneously supportive and judgmental. She's always been that way and, in defense, Janet has always sorted it out. *Or it will pass,* she added. *Most things do. Just keep in mind, you cannot mold a child as you molded clay.*

Janet bristled at the retort, despite its legitimacy. Long ago, and throughout her youth, she aspired to be a sculptor. She began with play dough, dabbled in mud and evolved to clay. She loved the dribs under her fingernails, the distinctive mineral scent. She kept a chisel close at hand, obsessed by the idea of manifesting something from nothing. She realized early on it would be too hard to make a living in fine art, so she flirted with a career in architecture, drawn to the elegance of design, but by the time she graduated college she was in debt. She seized an entry-level administrative position at the museum and discovered the pleasure of a calm workplace. Every day, even the busiest days, balancing the demands of members and patrons, planners and curators, she wanders into a gallery, absorbing artistic beauty as she once immersed herself in clay, and where she longs to be in the midst of these awful nights.

Twelve weeks pass with no respite. Melanie takes to sleeping three-hours midday, an olive branch, of sorts, when Janet might have rested, but as sleep-deprived and grumpy as she is, she is also restless. She digs out a drawing pad and sketches furiously, as if a mystical force has commandeered her hands. She produces a series of surreal Picasso-like images or hybrid forms with animal features, like Magritte. One day, she draws a charcoal portrait of spectral archangels in the throes of battle and they all share a disturbing resemblance to her daughter.

Despite, or because of the peculiarity of the drawings, Janet feels emboldened, like an explorer or an archeologist on the trail of discovery. Perhaps the images will evolve to three-dimensional and she might return to the clay, but each day, as the drawings take shape, Melanie wakes and Janet returns to mothering.

The next night, Janet doesn't close her eyes at all. She runs to Melanie at the first peep and goes through the steps. While awaiting the intensification, she gazes out the window to the full moon, a harvest moon, nearly orange, nearly consuming the sky. She implores the gods of exhausted mothers and terrorized children to save them. When Melanie wails again, Janet cannot sit there any longer. She bundles the child into a blanket and charges down the stairs to the back door, opens the garage and flops her into the car seat with the blanket tucked tightly around her from neck to toes.

Melanie's wide eyes open wider. She instantly stops crying and stares at her mother as intently as an owl might glare at an invader to the nest, and then, just as Janet believes they might have a bonding moment, releases a high-pitched wail.

Janet slams the door and slowly reverses the car out of the garage. The neighborhood is dark and still. Street lamps go off at midnight and few front door lights are lit. She drives toward Main Street where a screaming child is less likely to be heard, then parks a distance from the nearest lamppost and opens both rear windows an inch for fresh air. She steps out of the car, locks it, twice, to be sure, and walks to the corner, far enough for the sound of her daughter's cries to be hardly heard, but not out of sight, and crouches on the curb on wobbly legs like a drunk.

This was not the way it was supposed to be. While pregnant, she and Ron devoured parenting and child-development literature. They watched Sesame Street. They purchased a family home with a fenced yard and in walking distance to good schools. They were determined to shower their child with affection. Pave the way to a healthy productive life. Nothing could have prepared them for the night terrors, nor could Janet conceive of the animosity she might feel toward her precious firstborn.

She listens to her own breathing as she once listened underwater. She pictures bubbles rising to the surface, the flicker of sunlight above, but here, under a cloudy night sky, there is no path to the light. Hidden from her daughter's cries, from a crushing sense of failure, the stillness is suddenly terrifying, as if she's trapped below the water's surface and out of air. Or has her daughter suffocated? Abandoned to perish in the backseat of a parked car?

She dashes back to find Melanie sound asleep, her head tipped against the seat cushion and with one hand pressing a corner of the blanket to her cheek for comfort.

Someday you will hate me, Janet mutters as she climbs into the car. *Worse, you will fear me, but you won't know why, because you won't remember this, you will only know, deep down, I betrayed you in a moment of need. I failed you, sweet girl and, I fear I will fail you again and again.*

Janet drives home and parks in the driveway. Not wanting to disturb the child or incite another bout of hysteria, she reclines her seat, nearly flat, and turns on her side to face her daughter. They sleep until Melanie wakens, arching her body to stretch out the kinks, with no sign of antagonism or fear. Janet releases her from the seat and Melanie bounds into the house as if they have only been to the playground.

Ron is pacing the kitchen with cell phone in hand, so relieved to see his wife and baby safe, he falls to his knees.

What the hell did you do? he cries.

Janet shakes her head and murmurs an apology, as Ron hugs Melanie and lifts her into the highchair. He tosses cereal puffs on the tray and pours a Sippy cup of milk. Janet reaches for a bag of coffee beans from the cupboard to grind, but she is trembling so severely, Ron takes the bag and eases her into a chair.

Sit, he says, turning to retrieve a glass of juice for her.

Janet sips, then stands again to grab a bowl of blueberries from the refrigerator.

Sit, I said, Ron repeats, taking the food from her hand. *What happened?*

I took her for a drive and we fell asleep in the driveway. That's all. At least she slept.

Jan, this has got to stop. Now you're the one who's hysterical, you see that, right?

I couldn't handle another night of it. I have to try everything.

The doctor was clear there's little to be done; we have to get through this. She doesn't even know she's in distress.

I don't believe that. She must know.

Honey, this will pass, all things are only now…

Spare me the bromide, please. Fine in principle, not in practice.

Please, Jan, get a grip. This will end, eventually.

And what if it doesn't? Janet whimpers.

Maybe it's time to see a therapist, Ron says.

Janet ignores the remark.

Ron, if these terrors were induced by someone else, you know, if she were possibly abused and cried her eyes out every night, we would put a stop to it. We would save our child. This is traumatic – it's going to corrupt her worldview.

Jan, honey, she…

Listen to me. Her whole body shakes. She screams. She sobs. She says weird stuff. Something awful is happening to our daughter.

Do we need an exorcist? Ron asks, a comment meant to assuage the gravity of the conversation, but Janet considers the possibility.

Oh no! You don't think...

I was kidding!

Ron pulls her up and wraps his arms around her, and this sign of compassion undermines the last of Janet's self-control.

This is absolutely agonizing. What am I doing wrong?

Absolutely nothing! You, we, we're doing nothing wrong. It's just inexplicable. No rhyme or reason. Something she was born with, maybe a reaction to the environment.

Janet pulls from his embrace. *Oh my God! We should check for black mold. Lead paint?*

Okay, but we checked when we moved in. Everything we've read says this doesn't last long. It's one of those things beyond our control, and not the first, I'm sure.

Janet hangs her head, desolate, yet undeterred. She believes she is the one to unlock the secret, before she implodes, or worse, explodes in a way that will harm her child, and this likelihood is more and more present, more and more disturbing, and too horrible to confess. Is she meant to save her daughter from an unseen danger? Or is she the danger?

The coach has proposed one last-ditch sleep training, which necessitates five-minute bouts of crying between visits. Their instincts contradict, but they relent, smothering their ears with pillows. In just three minutes, however, Janet jumps up and runs down the hall, ignoring Ron's entreaties.

A siren rings out nearby. Police cars are rarely heard in this neighborhood and never in the middle of the night, a concession to the community in light of nearly empty streets for emergency vehicles to speed through. The alarm is an angry assault on sleepy ears, as jarring as Melanie's cries, and when Janet enters the nursery, Melanie is standing with her eyes wide open, clutching the crib railing, shouting. *Foo-egg-oh!*

More nonsense language, she thinks, although, perhaps, something to do with the beginner Legos Ron has brought home, building with Melanie floppy little creatures like dachshunds or trolls.

Foo-egg-oh! she repeats, her arms outstretched in desperation, and when Janet lifts her from the crib, Melanie grips her mother's neck with both hands, as if to strangle her. Janet feels the volcanic heat rising from her daughter's body. For a moment, she's afraid of her child. She jerks the girl's hands off her throat and carries her downstairs to the living room, hoping a change of scene might alleviate their mutual panic.

Janet's throat hurts, as if she too has nonsense words buried there. Her breathing is hard and fast. She feels the heat rising under her own skin. She wants to toss her daughter out a window. Suffocate her into silence. She is so terrified of what she may be capable of she starts back up the stairs to bring Melanie to Ron for safety. Melanie's cries suddenly cease and she curls her little body into Janet as if pleading, *please, don't give up on me*. They sit on the top stair, holding tightly to each other, bonded by misery, until Melanie falls asleep in her mother's arms and Janet returns her to the crib.

The next morning, she tells Ron about the sirens and the nonsensical word, and he alleges that Melanie may have graduated to real nightmares and these might prove more manageable. Janet is not appeased. She drops Melanie at Mrs. Angelos' place on her way to work and when she returns at the end of the day, the sitter, who has noticed the dark bags under Janet's eyes, the slumped shoulders and lumbering footsteps, invites her in for tea.

Within moments, Janet breaks down in tears and describes the situation. *It's so awful. She cries, she shouts, she babbles, she gazes into space like an alien!*

Mrs. Angelos makes a sign of the cross and brings her fingertips to her lips. *Dios mio*, she murmurs. She leans forward to embrace Janet, who collapses into her arms. After a short cry, Janet pulls away, ashamed of weakness. The pose of defeat.

I don't suppose anything like this ever happened to one of yours, she asks, swiping her tears away with the tissue Mrs. Angelos has handed to her.

Mrs. Angelos shifts from solemnity to a smile. *Similar, yes, one of them, yes.*

You're not sure which one?

Four children, born close together, those early years, they blur. I do remember now I wanted to smother her. Yes, that's it. Magdalena. The first girl. I thought she would be easy after the boys. She laughs.

Never easy, oh no. More than once, I handed her to my husband to keep her safe, from me!

Janet stares at Mrs. Angelos in shock.

Of course, you do not, do you? she assures Janet. *You want to, now and then. Sometimes in class, too, there was one I wanted to banish. No, you never give up. Not on a child. Even the most belligerent or restless children need us, yes? Maybe all the more.*

But you never want to strangle Melanie?

Oh no, this angel?

Not in the middle of the night, Janet mutters.

Mrs. Angelos nods. *This will pass.*

So my husband says, and the doctor says. Janet sighs. She's about to leave when she remembers what she wanted to ask. *Last night, she was shouting another strange word. I wonder if it's something you've heard. Sounds like foo-eggo. Ever hear her say that?*

Fuego? Mrs. Angelos says, with less emphasis on the g.

Yes, I mean, that's what it sounded like.

Fuego means fire. I speak Spanish to her at times, best to start young, but I don't think I've said that. She chuckles. *I must tell you, she may be a Mexican, I mean, in another life. One of us, si Niña?*

Melanie climbs into her lap and nestles there.

Janet is incredulous.

There were sirens last night, but is she old enough to connect sirens to fire?

Toys have sirens. Books too, Mrs. Angelos says. *And these little ones, they learn fast. Or...*

What?

Maybe she experienced a fire in another life.

How do you mean?
Maybe she died in a fire.
Mrs. Angelos again makes the sign of the cross.
You believe that sort of thing?
Oh yes. Not you?
I'm a Catholic. We go to heaven, end of story.
Mrs. Angelos breaks into laughter. *I too am Catholic, but I believe we carry the past with us into our future. And the babies, they are closer to their pasts. Closer to the angels that guide them to new life. They haven't had time to let go.*

Janet is shocked. She's never been spiritual by nature, or mystical. She's no fan of magical realism in fiction. She prefers representational art to the abstract. She believes, she needs to believe, in the concrete.

She dismisses the thought. This cannot be.

Tonight, however, contemplating the concept of a previous life tormenting her daughter, she cannot sleep at all. When Melanie wakes up screaming, she lifts her from the crib and carries her to the window to gaze at the sliver of a moon. Janet knows little of astronomy and takes no interest in astrology; however, in that moment, she considers the cyclical nature of the moon, the cycle of all living things – a reminder there is renewal in what seems to conclude.

Look, Mel, she says. *The beauty of the night sky. The moon, the stars, the galaxy, so bright, so clear, yet distant and majestic. The gods worshipped the night sky. Sailors use stars to navigate. Farmers follow the seasons to plant. All part of who we are, where we go and how we grow. Nothing to fear.*

Melanie continues sobbing. Her body quivers, her head shifts side to side as if rejecting an inner command.

She's just a child, Janet argues with herself. She has to repress her rage, but she fears this might be the night: the night she will demand acquiescence. She is at her wit's end. She cannot go on.

As if reading her mind, Melanie's body stiffens. She flexes her feet, kicking Janet hard in the belly, and as they start to keel over, Janet rights them just in time and flops into the rocking chair – pain, fatigue, despair, taking their toll. She cries, the two weeping together as one, and when Janet regains control to stand, as she heads toward the crib for safekeeping, Melanie clings to her as if otherwise she might drown, and all the while mumbling a series of syllables with clipped consonants and vowel endings that sound like Spanish.

Is it conceivable Mrs. Angelos was right? Janet wonders. Disbelieving, and desperate, she reaches into her memory for high school Spanish.

Todo esta bien, sweetheart. All is well.

Beyond a thin stream of tears and dwindling shudders, Melanie grows still. She seems to be listening.

Todo esta bien, Janet repeats.

The child calms in her mother's arms.

Te quiero, Janet whispers. *I love you. Your mother loves you.*

Melanie lowers her head to Janet's shoulder and closes her eyes, and, although Janet will wonder if she imagined so, she feels her daughter's body release some weight, as if a spirit has been set free.

Todo esta bien, Janet repeats, as she drops again into the chair, holding and rocking her daughter until she sleeps. Janet holds her tightly and stays in place. Together they rest until daylight floods the nursery, when the child slips from her mother's arms to drag a few toys from the toy basket to the carpet.

Janet is smiling and Melanie playing when Ron enters the room.

What's up? he asks.

Esta bien, Janet answers.

Esta bien? What's with the Spanish?

Melanie looks up at her father and nods her head yes, with a bright smile, and in that smile, Janet sees more than relief; she sees the delight of conquest.

The sculptor has been sculpted.

A Righteous Woman

A heavyset security guard stands on the far side of the surveillance scanner. Two buttons on his blue uniform shirt are being tugged open from his heft, exposing a ribbon of white T-shirt. He wears a similarly disheveled expression as he rubs his hands together so hard and fast he might be hoping for fire.

The courthouse should be warmer than the damp cold this winter day. I imagine the rusted pipes in these old municipal buildings are not up to the task, like the cranky radiators in my apartment that groan when called to service. A huge fan hangs high from the rotunda in a pointless attempt to circulate warmer air that has risen to the peak.

On the other hand, the chill may be by design: no one in this place is meant to feel comfortable.

Move along, the guard murmurs reflexively to each of us passing through.

I assume most of this herd plans to defend themselves, as I am, although some may have been called to appear on behalf of someone else. No other reason to enter this austere building with inhospitably hard marble floors and drafty hallways.

Some of these people must be thieves or embezzlers, maybe murderers or pedophiles. A deeply disturbing thought. I'm headed to traffic court, where I will be deemed guilty or innocent for a minor violation. I suspect few people argue speeding tickets, certainly not people of means. Why waste the time? I work part-time now, so I have the time to dispute this overpriced ticket. More to the point, my integrity has been assailed. I am a woman of principle, my friends and family will attest to this, and although a highway patrol officer says I was driving well beyond the speed limit, I was raised, and raised my children, to stand up when our honor is besmirched. If we cannot or do not, who will?

From security I am pointed in the direction of a metal stanchion where the courtrooms are listed, some on this floor, most upstairs, with the starting time for today's docket. I'm to appear in number seven, a lucky number in games of luck. Also seven days in the week. Seven continents. God rested on the seventh day. This bodes well.

I follow the arrows down a long wide hallway. Mostly men mill about, prosecutors and lawyers likely, all wearing dark suits, attaché cases at their feet and file folders clutched to their chests, deep in conversation in surreptitious tones. Assistants or advisors hover nearby like puppies for their supper. They warm their hands on coffee cups from vending machines lining the corridor. The aroma calls to me, but I doubt I am permitted to bring food or drink with me and it seems imperative, especially today, to play by the rules.

Hearing rooms, they are called, not courtrooms. I've never been in one of these, although several times I've spent the day at this very courthouse awaiting jury selection. I've not yet been impaneled. Twice I came close and looked forward to the chance to participate in our judicial system, but both times, as is typical, I'm told, the case concluded with a plea bargain before trial. Was justice served?

On entering Hearing Room #7 I am battered by warm stagnant air, a stark contrast to the cold corridor. Tall multi-pane windows along one wall, with bars on the outside, may not have been opened in a century. An odor of stress – sweat, cortisol, adrenaline – clogs the ventilation and a hint of ammonia wafts from the dingy floors. The air is thick with apprehension, or is it resignation? Like the dust under a bed we ignore until it creeps between our toes.

People sit rigidly. They line up in neat rows like kindergarten children instructed to wait quietly for snack. Most are brown or black, very few Asians, although many reside in this city. Are they so obedient they scrupulously obey the law? Or, even if unjustly accused, are they so intimidated by authority they do not appeal?

I am a definite oddball here. The sole person in the room who does not belong, like the game I played long ago with my kids – which item does not belong with the others? Me, I want to shout. I do not belong with these others! A Caucasian woman, well-educated and fit, wearing expensive gray wool slacks and a black cashmere sweater, with a two-hundred dollar silk scarf fashioned around my neck and designer suede boots, accessorized with understated top drawer gold jewelry. Here, in New York City, the so-called melting pot, or what some call the salad bowl, I still have an advantage. I expect to be treated differently by virtue of race and staging – presumed innocent, which we should all be until proven guilty.

Artificial light spills from cork ceiling panels, flattening human shapes to two-dimensional and further squashing the spirit. Like the vise on the table saw my great grandfather once used to secure a sheet of lumber. He had been trained in Italy as a cabinetmaker before he migrated, and then, snared by the Great Depression, took whatever work he could find, often demeaning odd jobs at the mill. In those days, a man of the trade worked his trade, a matter of self-respect and, as a result of his dedication, six children, fifteen grandchildren and twenty-two great-grandchildren inherited mahogany, walnut, oak or cherry bookshelves, chests with brass pulls or tables with mother of pearl inlay. I still pay bills at an oversized desk with beveled edges and I picture my father there studying paperwork for one or another of the projects he managed once he ascended from construction worker to contractor.

Today, in the courthouse, the image of the vise reminds me of what those heinous film villains use for torture, the sort of pivotal scene when music elevates to a crescendo and the camera zooms to a terrified victim before fading to black. No fading to black in Hearing Room #7.

Mounted on three walls, thick with many coats of grayed white paint, black signs with white stick-on letters in English and Spanish demand attention.

IDENTIFICATION REQUIRED AT ALL TIMES.

NO FOOD OR DRINK ALLOWED.

TURN OFF ALL RADIOS, PHONES AND BEEPERS.

No one uses beepers anymore, I might point out, or portable radios for that matter. However this place, with its harsh light, sterile walls and cautionary signs is intended to silence. That's the one sign missing, although inherently clear: *DO NOT SPEAK UNTIL SPOKEN TO.*

There are also signs displaying the universal red circle with a slash through a cigarette, as if anyone would dream of lighting up here. Everyone knows by now smoking is not permitted in city buildings, only on sidewalks, in doorways, driveways and alleys, where a haze gathers like tiny tornadoes assaulting passers-by. I quit smoking years ago, before the children were born, but sometimes I march into that trail of smoke and inhale deeply with pleasure.

The hearing room is snug, not so much discreet as stifling, and nothing like the imposing setting on television or film. The camera conjures formidability. In this courtroom, eight rows of chairs are lined up like pews in a chapel. At front, the judge's bench is elevated by one steep step, partly concealed by a wooden frame, mahogany, I think, creating a dry moat between judge and those awaiting judgment. Intimidating, of course.

No matter the small scale or sterility, I suddenly feel vulnerable, like a child facing an angry parent or a bully on the playground. The thought has not occurred to me until this moment that I may be ill equipped to face condemnation.

To release nervous tension, I take a headcount in the room. Thirty-two people are here. Some may be family members, maybe advocates or translators. Several fan themselves using postcards they received to confirm attendance, while others sit seemingly unperturbed. Perhaps they've been here before and they know the ropes. They flip through magazines or newspapers. A middle-aged woman opens a library book and I lean forward to see what's she's reading, but cannot make out the title. I suppose I should have brought a book, although I'm far too jittery to read.

More signs: *DO NOT INTERFERE WITH CAMERAS OR RECORDING DEVICES IN OPERATION.*

PROPER ATTIRE REQUIRED.

VESTIRSE APPROPRIADO SE REQUIERE.

Sounds so much friendlier in Spanish, I think, as I scan the seats – all taken except in one totally empty section on the far side. Why do they cluster in one area when there are seats? As I squeeze along a row to get there, people move their legs to make room, although few make eye contact. Do they fear guilt might be contagious?

A compact black man dressed in a pink shirt and a navy tie rubs a handkerchief over his brow. As I pass, he smiles and shrugs his shoulders, as if he wants to share his embarrassment at being here. A plump brown woman in a wrinkled blouse and tight skirt holds a toddler in her lap and grips the hand of a preschooler seated next to her. She seems to want to protect them even as she clings to them. Perhaps she hopes to reflect their youthful innocence. Anyone can see she's not a danger to society.

A petite woman with copper skin and cropped black hair looks up to me. Her mouth is slightly open, but no smile. Her teeth are small and crooked and her lips are cracked. She is Chinese. I cannot explain exactly how I know she is of Chinese origin and not from Japan or Taiwan or one of the Southeast Asian countries, I just know. Some years ago, when I visited Hong Kong, with my husband, all the women there, also short and black-haired, seemed perpetually rushed. They moved in packs, as if they existed only within a crowd. I would like to ask her if she is accused of speeding or if she drove through a stop sign or failed to signal a turn, the stupid stuff people are ticketed for.

Seriously, there are far more important things for police to attend to.

I park in a seat near the far aisle, in the second row, close enough to see and hear and rise when called upon, but not too conspicuous, I hope, and only then I see another sign: *RESERVED FOR POLICE.* When I look around again, two people leaning against the wall glare at me. Who do you think you are? they must be thinking, although I'm sure they would agree that all of us should be shown the courtesy of a seat while we wait. As there are no police here yet, I stay put. If I'm booted out, I will say I did not notice the sign. Mea culpa. In truth, I feel safer here. Insulated from the others.

As a child, I looked up to the police in my neighborhood. Their buttons gleamed in the sun like shining armor. I was taught men in blue are our friends. Protectors. Saviors. I still believe they mean to be. On the other hand, one has only to watch the evening news to suspect otherwise. Power corrupts. The few demean the many, although my mother used to say the rotten apple doesn't ruin the barrel. In this millennium, everything is different for law enforcement. Social media and public outrage make it harder for rotten apples to hide. All the more reason to be here – each of us must defend even the most trivial trampling on our rights, even speeding tickets.

Ironically, I don't drive much anymore. Not since I moved back to the city from the suburbs. My kids wanted me to keep the family home forever, but I missed city life. This is my comfort zone and I prefer public transportation. I rent a car now and then, only for short holidays.

The morning of the alleged offense, I was on my way to Greenport, on the north fork of Long Island, where an old friend was spending a few weeks in a bright white house with a view of the water. I was cruising along, pleased at the blessedly light traffic, listening to a podcast in which a renaissance man studies a subject in-depth and invites an expert in the field to confirm or deny. That day they were discussing mosaics. Apparently the art form is back in fashion. Mosaics, I learned, originated in Mesopotamia, in the 3rd millennium BC. They used seashells and stones that must have taken a few thousand years to ground down, when someone had the brilliant idea to gather them to represent a moment or a scene. Podcasts make driving long distances infinitely more pleasant and I was listening intently.

The posted speed limit was 65 mph and everyone around me was going roughly 75 mph, so I maintained the pace, which seems prudent on highway drives. Fairly often, faster cars passed in the left lane, so when a police car's spinning lights trailed behind me, I assumed he was after another driver. When he stayed on my tail, I pulled over. I imagined a broken rear light or an out-of-date registration sticker, or something similarly harmless, but he alleged I was driving 81 mph. I responded, respectfully, I was sure I was not. He said he clocked me with radar.

Sixteen miles over the limit, he insisted.

I might have asked, why me? Why not the guy in the Mercedes who passed me at breakneck speed a few miles back? Still, respecting the law, I held my tongue. I also wasn't sure how to dispute the radar.

When the officer returned my license and registration, and handed me the ticket, he said, *drive carefully and have a safe trip.*

I was furiously mute, and when he drove away, outraged by the exorbitant fee, I had the inclination to speed the rest of the way. After all, lightning does not strike twice, but I guess I was shaken by the incident, as I stayed in the slow lane.

My friend said I should appeal. *If everyone was at the same speed, you must have been singled out. He may have had a quota to fill and you were a random target*, she posited.

I didn't feel like I had broken a law or at least I wasn't the only one. I certainly hadn't committed a serious offense. I don't want the ticket on my record – I have a squeaky clean driving record. An excellent credit score for that matter. I pay my taxes on time. I'm kind to my neighbors. I rarely scolded my kids and never cheated on my husband. A model citizen! Why let one ticket ruin that?

So here I sit, prepared to mount a challenge to what is more likely a foregone conclusion.

My stomach is churning. Why am I so nervous about a stupid ticket? What else might I be accused of? Have they lured me here with a trumped up charge to demand atonement? We are all guilty of something. There are no innocents in this world, except newborns. The judge may suddenly stand, thrust out his arm and point to me, shouting *there she is!* Will I have to confess my trespasses, as minor as they are?

Okay. I squash spiders with glee, they give me the shivers. When a sales clerk makes an error in my favor, I don't always make good – her mistake, not mine. I tell little white lies to spare feelings or keep the peace. Don't we all? Dishonest, sure, but not illegal. Yet here, surrounded by scofflaws and malcontents, I feel like the only one in Hearing Room #7 who may be rightfully charged.

In the spirit of confession, I'm also guilty of breaking and entering. Long ago, in adolescence, I was determined to win a piano competition that, in hindsight, I had little chance of winning. My parents had an old upright with sticky keys, badly in need of tuning, so every afternoon the week before the concert, I snuck into an upstairs apartment to practice on a baby grand. The neighbors worked and their kids were in college, so their place was empty. And, because I occasionally dallied with their youngest son, I knew where the key was hidden. The music he played on my body the summer before might have been classified a misdemeanor. I suppose I felt justified. The walls in those old city buildings are so thick, no one would hear.

Now and then, frustrated by my fumbling fingers, I took a break from practice and prowled their apartment, sniffing perfume bottles and scented soaps and trying on jewelry from a box tucked into the top drawer of a lingerie chest. I found a wad of bills buried in a sock on an upper shelf of a closet, but I left it there. I pocketed four quarters sitting idly on a dresser and the following day, I put them back in exactly the same place. On a lark, I took a few books, I still have them: Balzac and Dostoyevsky, writers my parents would not own. I remember trembling at my audacity, not with fear or guilt, oh no. More like the delighted quivering of a young woman at the first touch of a seduction. Not a criminal. Deliciously wicked, with a sublime sense of impunity. No one ever knew.

Six police officers enter the hearing room at once and I jump up with an apologetic expression and make my way across the room to lean against a wall. A tall black man with nearly white hair offers me his chair. I decline. *In case I want to make a quick exit,* I quip. He smiles. Must be hard to be elderly and black and have to fight a ticket you received probably because you were profiled. Now that's a crime.

From this vantage point, the pews, filled with solemn faces, seem holy. The police, in contrast, like the military. The effect of that sea of blue, even that small sea, is daunting. They remove their iconic NYPD caps and scrutinize the paperwork in their hands. I don't recognize my accuser, but I encountered him just the once. I wonder if they hate this part of the job. The need to justify their indictments must grate at their sense of power, as polished as their buttons. On the other hand, they might enjoy a respite from regular duty. Perhaps I'm doing him a favor by being here.

The judge enters, we all stand, the bailiff asks us all at once to raise hands and swear an oath to tell the truth. The proceedings begin.

A tall brown man wearing an oversized sports jacket and faded jeans is up first. His English is broken, his voice guttural, as if he has spent too much of his life trying to be heard. The judge calls for a translator and tables his case. Another policeman stands with the next defendant, a slight black man who stares at his sneakers, as if, by not looking up, he might seem the victim. His previous misdemeanors, rather a long list, insinuate guilt before the officer recites the charges. His license will be revoked and he will pay a hefty fine. The judge tells him this is the last time. He had best not show up in his court again or face jail time.

I'm pleased by this, believing the more people ahead of me pronounced guilty improves my odds, like one of those standardized tests where you fill in a circle of the multiple choice options – just so many a, b or c answers.

Another man stands up. He speaks so softly I cannot make out the gist of his case. The judge asks the officer two questions, which I also cannot make out, but he answers no to both. All the police follow their responses by saying, *your honor*. Nothing like a sign of respect to smooth out the edges of a dispute. The judge asks another question, nods, mutters something about a technicality, which the officer acknowledges with a disappointed nod, and the judge waves the man toward the resolution window.

What sort of technicality negates guilt? I will ask Google, although too late now to sort that out.

Two more cases are quickly dispatched before another young man approaches the bench with an older burly bald man, likely a lawyer. A policewoman stands. The three face the judge like the holy trinity. The judge listens with a blank expression on his face as the policewoman fills in the details. That's the extent of this: no trial in the hearing room, no jury, and no option for the accused beyond this one white aging man with a weary poker face and, I suspect, a hardened heart.

This realization, more than anything else in this stuffy room, is frightening. My fate is in the hands of one being and all my life I believed my fate was in my own hands.

I feel suddenly as helpless as I felt when I was a lonely child lost in the middle of five siblings, and still, all these years later, when I trip on the sidewalk or the stairs and land too hard. Or when one of my kids is struggling at work or with a partner and I can do nothing for them. The way I felt when my mother, then my father, my favorite brother and then my husband, lay dying.

This sense of frailty, this is the power of the court. We alone know our guilt or innocence and most of us, I'm certain, find ourselves wanting, even if innocent of this particular charge.

Is it possible the judge will figure out I'm to blame for something far more contemptible? I would plead for mercy. I was coerced as a child, your honor, I would say, long before a simple trespass to play piano or subsequent infringements of etiquette. Imprinted, in effect, to crime.

Consider this, I would explain. I was ten years old when I was dispatched for the summer to a camp upstate where bright stars illumined the night skies and the days were structured dawn to dusk. My parents emptied their rainy day jar to send me away from another summer spent meandering with a pack of neighborhood miscreants. The older siblings worked for my father, the younger were happy on playgrounds. I was clearly a nuisance. At camp, I learned to dive off a dock into a pristine lake, silky water so cold I shivered before I landed, savoring the moment afterward when I wrapped myself in a beach towel to dry in the sun. I played baseball on a field instead of stickball in an empty lot and I hiked lush hillsides inhaling mountain air as desperately as if I'd just been born.

The last week of camp, eighty campers were divided into two teams – red and blue, the camp colors – in an annual three-day competition called Color War, before such a term would be deleted from the lexicon. We ran relay races, jumped hurdles, competed in dodgeball, basketball, baseball and archery, and the ever-popular boisterous tug-of-war. The competition concluded with a parade: campers in costume shouting group cheers and singing rollicking team songs with original lyrics composed to show tunes or rock music.

Color War had been especially close that year and came down to the final parade. My team, the Cherokees, was ahead of the Blue Waves by a narrow margin. One of the team generals, an aspiring artist, sketched a rendering of an Indian reservation for the banner, and the more artistic campers, charged with bringing the banner to life, requested additional paint, also decorative supplies like fabric marker, embroidery thread, colorful beads and baubles. However, as the budget had been shot on materials for hackneyed Indian headdresses, desperate measures were required. Under the auspices of a competitive team captain, a contingent was dispatched to scavenge for supplies in the small town nearby. Because all campers were required to participate in Color War, I was, reluctantly I imagine, tapped for the mission with an older camper. We piled into a jeep for the short bumpy ride to the mercantile, a general store with an eclectic array of merchandise. Counselors entered first to canvas the store and spent their last cash on a few tubes of paint.

Back at the jeep, we were prepped on the fine art of shoplifting. I hadn't known what would be asked of me and, once briefed, even at that tender age, I knew I was the right choice, because I was then, and still, the sort of person who exudes innocence. I look people in the eye and speak clearly, as I was taught to do. I never raise my voice or overstep my bounds. I'm affable, not officious. Short and slight, I fancy the notion I could slip between shadows, like Peter Pan.

My partner in crime, a pretty brunette with sun-pinked skin and a face filled with freckles, was strikingly cavalier. I wanted to be just as cool, although I was astounded by what I was being asked to do. Also as enthralled as I'd ever been, despite a sharp thumping at pulse points and an ominous tingling down my spine.

My parents would have been appalled. I would have been beaten with a belt and shunned for weeks for sullying family values. My siblings and I had been inculcated from birth in the absolute necessity of honesty and decency, values crucial to Italian immigrants trying to rise above disparaging Mafia stereotypes. Yet, there I was, more than willing to betray family values and certain I was up to the task.

The tall handsome Color War captain pulled his sweatshirt over my head to below my hips. I remember the subtle scent of male body odor that was, for a pre-pubescent, delectable. I felt like Cinderella with a glass slipper – totally smitten with him and with my new exalted self-image. He pointed out two deep pockets along each side and a hidden pocket tucked on the underside.

Just in case, he said, with a kiss to my forehead for good luck. I'm sure I swooned.

We entered the store. My compatriot distracted the clerk at the register with a barrage of questions about the more expensive merchandise and hunting rifles behind the counter, while I skulked around the store, fascinated by the displays of everything from screwdrivers and windshield wiper blades to dishcloths and gardening gloves. I was fingering a pile of white handkerchiefs with scalloped edges when a bell rang over the front door and I turned to see a dark-haired woman wearing blue jeans and a plaid shirt, the sleeves rolled up to her elbow and the collar open to a V-neck, like a cowgirl. She made her way down the aisle where I stood and stopped right in front of me.

What a lovely thing, a handkerchief, she mused. *So much nicer than a tissue.*

I looked up at her and purred similarly, *my mother would love these.*

She smiled. *Some of these city kids are so sweet,* she called to the clerk and he nodded absentmindedly.

They must have assumed we were as guileless as their children and, in the moment, I felt ashamed of what I was there to do, but also renewed determination, if only to prove myself above these country bumpkins.

I headed straight for the back wall. I slipped packages of red felt and gold tacks into the side pockets. What a rush! I pocketed a packet of reflective decals and a couple of tubes of glue. Mission accomplished. Nevertheless, in thrall to the persona of a thief, I slipped a couple of thimbles of shiny thread and a small can of yellow paint into the inside pocket. If I'd had more pockets, I would have taken more. I crossed my arms over my belly as if in pain and made my way to the exit, grumbling to my compatriot that our camp counselor was waiting. I remember the man at the counter smiled kindly and I felt another pang of guilt as I waited at the door while she purchased a pack of gum for the sake of legitimacy.

We strolled out of the store and down the stairs, as I innately understood only the guilty would hustle.

Some time later, the proprietor may have noticed a glitch in the inventory, although I doubt it. No computers. No surveillance cameras. So little was missing, none the wiser. And that was the day I learned, confirmed many times since that without witness, there is no crime. In effect, never happened.

Once safely back at the jeep parked around the corner, out of sight of the store, my cohort told the others I was a star. *A natural,* she said proudly.

I beamed with pride as I climbed into the jeep, my hands still spread over the pockets to protect the treasure. Everyone was pleased with my performance and I recall to this day feeling the sort of significance I had no idea I craved. I also remember thinking my parents were mistaken – crime pays. No one was hurt. No harm done.

A few years after that, soon after the piano trespass, I stole a candy bar. Some time later: socks. Lipsticks. I fed myself through college on ramen noodle and cereal boxes slipped into my book bag. I filched a silk scarf to wear on my first date with the man I married and have since dressed up my wardrobe with bits and bobs I could never otherwise afford, like the scarf and bracelet I wear today. I told my husband I shop the sale racks and he applauded my economy, which was the truth, because the less I spent on me, the more I had for the family.

I never lifted anything for anyone else, so as not to taint them with stolen goods. No, I do this for me. It's not the stuff, it's the thrill. The same kick I suspect Wall Street wheeler-dealers, real estate magnates and politicians thrive on. And the thing is, since that first time, I've never felt felonious, not in the act or in the aftermath, because, like most white-collar criminals, I've not been caught.

I do occasionally feel shame and sitting here, before the judge, I realize I'm due for a comeuppance. This may be the ticket, so to speak, although I'm less in need of justice as absolution, as if I've inadvertently stepped into a confessional, which I never do, seeking penance for all my trespasses.

My number is called and the bailiff confirms my name, faltering on the pronunciation. I don't correct him. I step forward, but at that moment the judge is approached by a clerk and raises his palm to us to wait. I'm not sure whether I should sit back down, so I remain standing, trapped between the judge and the blue sea of police seated behind me. Caught in the glare of the headlights, so to speak. I try to breathe slowly, to stay calm and avoid an appearance of guilt. I hear the rustling of papers and scattered coughing in the pews, sounds that grate on the nerves, but I don't move a muscle.

So much is at stake at this moment, more than I could have imagined when I passed through security an hour ago.

The clerk recedes as silently as she arrived and the judge waves me forward. He scans the complaint against me.

Do you want a lawyer? he asks in a flat voice. He glances up without actually looking at me.

No, your honor, I answer.

Where is the officer? he asks the bailiff.

The officer's name is called. No answer. The bailiff shifts his weight from one side to the other and the linoleum floor cracks underfoot. This floor, like the defendants, has been stripped of its shine. The officer is called again. Apparently he's not here. He may be ill, I suppose, or may have had something more pressing.

If I took the time to defend this charge, the officer should be here. *No fair*, I almost cry, like a child playing a street game.

The judge nods with a sigh and stamps the paperwork. *Charge dismissed.*

Your honor, I have something to say, I respond, my voice loud, urgent, although my body trembles, my heart rumbles in my chest, as I face this elder, another of the many elders over time who have commandeered my fate.

He frowns at me. *Something to say? Unless you want to plead guilty, move on.*

I freeze for a second. Should I confess? Should I pay the ticket? Seems a trifling penalty for a lifetime of misdemeanors. On the other hand, why should I?

No, thank you, sorry, your honor, I stammer.

Go figure, the judge says to the bailiff, who shakes his head and points me to the window as he calls the next case.

I ask the clerk at the window what happened, but she says she has no clue and hands me a receipt. I don't even glance at the paper. I fold it in half and then again in half and press it into my purse as a memento.

On the way out, I approach one of the lawyers. *A quick question, please*, I interrupt, and although he is clearly pressed for time, I describe what happened.

What does it mean? I ask.

Citation officer has to show up. If he's not here to stand up for the charge, no charge.

He turns back to the matter at hand and I touch his arm.

So, I'm innocent, I pronounce more than ask.

The lawyer locks eyes with mine. He, like the judge, has seen it all. He says with a knowing smirk on his face, *charge dismissed means no charge. Not the same as innocent.*

I take a deep breath and as casually as possible stroll out of Hearing Room #7, down the stairs and out of the courthouse, just the way I sauntered from the mercantile all those years ago, and still do, now and then, from one shop or another with this or that hidden in my purse or pockets.

No one the wiser. No harm done.

A Reluctant Traveler

On the morning of her fourth day in Paris, midway through a trip she never meant to take, Ellen awakened to slivers of light seeping through a flimsy window shade into her hotel room, light drawn back into darkness by merlot red walls. The small room was three times longer than wide, one window with rusted hinges at the short end. A narrow bed, with a carved iron headboard, pressed its length against a long wall, next to a small wood table marred with overlapping glass stains. The one ornamentation, a black framed print on the wall opposite the bed, depicted in bold colors the face of a woman with triangular eyes, a radically stretched jawline and jagged teeth, as if a student rendering of a Picasso. Facing the door, in lieu of a closet, a short pole held three empty hangers. Ellen had never unpacked – at the end of each day she shoved dirty clothes into a plastic bag she'd tucked on the shelf above the hangers and folded the clean to wear again.

Two stars, one step above a hostel, was the average hotel rating posted on a budget travel website, which Ellen thought fitting, as she might be described the same.

She roused herself to squeeze her squat body into the phone booth-sized stall shower, shivering between droplets of tepid water and longing for a hot bath home in Philadelphia. Then she hurriedly dressed to get to the first floor dining room on time, having missed the first complimentary breakfasts in favor of sleep. She has never traveled out of the country before and had not anticipated the intensity of jetlag, slogging through days and tossing through nights.

When she arrived downstairs, the six breakfast tables were occupied and she hesitated, not wanting to miss another free meal, a rich coffee aroma further enticement to stay. She stepped back, out of the way, leaning against the banister at the stair landing to wait. No one noticed. Ellen is not one to incite interest – she generally fades into her environs. In Paris, however, she felt exposed, as if her cloak of invisibility had been ripped away.

She hoped no one heard her stomach rumbling as she gazed beyond the diners to a grimy Palladian window overlooking Place Dauphine, at the tip of the Ile de la Cité, a strip of land floating in the River Seine, and near Pont Neuf, the oldest of the standing bridges ironically named the new. Surrounding this square are typically Parisian apartment buildings with stone roofs and elongated windows bordered by intricately carved moldings. At street level, cafés take in their tables and chairs near midnight and set them out again after sunrise, as if opening and closing the day.

A burly man chomping a baguette and scanning his iPad looked up and waved in such a welcoming way he might have been awaiting her arrival. She couldn't imagine he meant her and, when she didn't respond, he beckoned again, doggedly. Ellen, despite her hunger, considered skipping breakfast entirely rather than face the obligatory etiquette of conversation. When he pointed with authority to the chair opposite him, the one empty chair in the room – a command to sit, not an invitation – Ellen sat.

Thank you, she murmured, without making eye contact. When he nodded and returned to his reading, she was relieved she might dine quietly after all.

A white porcelain cup and saucer appeared before her, filled with steaming black coffee. Ellen loves hot coffee. She drinks two large mugs, black, every morning, and decaf after midday in order to avoid caffeine overdrive. The waitress, wearing a short black apron and a frayed expression, made another pass, barely stopping as she plopped on the table a red plastic basket containing one-half baguette and a golden brioche, with a crock of pale butter. The same basket perched on every table. Continental breakfast now defined.

Ellen floated one hand over the basket, savoring the warmth, before examining an assortment of tiny marmalade jars on the table. She chose orange, with slivers of rind, which she spread generously over a chunk of the softened butter on a thick slice of the bread, crunching the first mouthful and washing it down with a long swill of coffee. If she had been alone, she would have sighed with satisfaction.

Soon after, when she signaled for a refill, the waitress scowled. Another horrid impatient American, Ellen imagined her thinking, even as she filled her cup to the brim. Of course Ellen would be recognized as American: pale freckled skin, perky nose, blue eyes, and flat brown hair with bangs cut across her forehead as if with garden shears. She wore plain loose-fitting jeans, white sneakers embossed with a Nike wave logo, purchased for the trip, and a navy cotton crewneck sweater. Ellen always wears comfortable clothes, ready-to-wear. Decidedly not French.

Her companion, his eyes focused on the iPad, one thick pointer finger swiping rapidly right to left, looked up with a broad smile. *Nothing like that first cup of coffee, which always demands a second*, he remarked.

He spoke English with a northern Pacific or Canadian accent, Ellen wasn't certain, although she has a talent for identifying accents, the result of a lifelong devotion to the stories of Sherlock Holmes, who always spotted the clues to the language of origin. She still enjoys the British black and white films of the great detective starring Basil Rathbone, to her mind closer to the genuine article than all the others, and she feels a special kinship to the iconic sleuth, because Ellen too is an observer of life, rather than a participant.

What brings you to Paris? he asked, *although one only has to spend time in this great city to realize the only reason to come to Paris is Paris, oui?*

He had the enthusiasm of a young man, despite signs of middle age: a close-cropped graying beard, scattered wrinkles and deeply carved frown lines. His thinning hair was mostly gray, like the beard, and he wore rimless glasses through which large dark eyes seemed drawn on his face, almost as two-dimensional as the Picasso-like print in her room. He too wore plain jeans, with a plaid flannel shirt, like a lumberjack, and tan leather boots with thick serrated soles, ideal for walking cobblestone streets.

Something about him – the intensity of focus, the rounded shoulders – suggested a task-oriented person, a person who meticulously pursues a sequence to its end, the means of equal or greater significance than the outcome. A mathematician, perhaps, she mused. Or an insurance analyst who measures lives on an actuarial table. Maybe a programmer. Someone, like Ellen, who adheres to a linear path.

She ignored his rhetorical question because Paris was nothing like the majestic city she had expected. Imposing in architecture and rich in history, yes; otherwise a gray palette of gray buildings under gray skies. The air too seemed gray, thick with soot and cigarette smoke. Even the pervasive scent of pastry and perfume could not sweeten the pungency. And when, during these first few days, morning haze dissipated to reveal an afternoon blue sky, to her eye, stone bridges and quays along the river reflected merely a more luminous gray.

Ellen's mother used to say Parisians had a reputation for arrogance. Haughty, was her word, uttered admiringly, not derisive, and now it occurred to Ellen a smug expression may be the best antidote to the burden of gray. Wasn't this supposed to be the city of light? The city of love? Not that it mattered. She traveled here only by entreaty. She would soon fulfill her obligation and return home to her simple life and Paris would be nothing more than a notion.

What surprised Ellen about the city was the symmetry – alleys, avenues and boulevards radiating from landmarks rising above the city like sound waves. A well-balanced infrastructure that belied its bohemian reputation. The River Seine, gunmetal gray and murky, carved the city into right and left embankments, insinuating balance, like an urban ledger. This she appreciated.

She swallowed bread and coffee in silence. Not one to say much, she often spends whole weekends mute, so when she speaks again on Monday mornings, her voice seems to emanate from someone else. On the other hand, she has an expansive and sophisticated vocabulary, the result of obsessive studies throughout elementary and middle school years for the annual spelling bee, the one and only occasion on which she excelled. An exalted vocabulary proved reason enough to eschew conversation, although Ellen never thinks of herself as superior in any way.

Magnificent city, is it not? her companion inquired again, and now Ellen felt obliged to answer.

This is my first trip...

Oh you will return, I promise you. Just like Bogey, remember?

He referred to the film *Casablanca*, Ellen knew, so she anticipated the recitation that followed.

We'll always have Paris, he intoned, in a pedestrian imitation of Humphrey Bogart.

Not wanting to disabuse him of enthusiasm, Ellen did not say that she thought Paris must be an acquired taste and she would never return. She took her last bite of breakfast and swallowed the last drop of coffee. When she stood, he too stood, extending his hand. She responded with a meager handshake and murmured thanks, and fled.

Ellen's mother should have been the one to travel to Paris. She inhabited a gray life, but dreamed in color. She was enamored of all things French, referring to herself as a Francophile. She listened to audio language lessons every day while preparing dinner, mimicking cadence and inflection aloud, and she gave every meal a dollop of cream or butter, a dose of lemon or wine, like Julia Child. She had a few dollars tucked away, but she never traveled, not even day trips, and Ellen never knew why, although her father worked two jobs all his life and of her mother's few friends, none seemed adventurous. Instead, she filled their house with cheaply framed Baroque prints and ruffled lampshades dabbed with Chanel cologne, and she incessantly listened to the music of Edith Piaf and Michel LeGrand.

Ellen made the trip to satisfy her mother's last request. She tried to convince herself no one would know if she reneged, but a promise is a promise. She planned an agenda using itineraries in the guides stacked by her mother's bedside, constructing a tour of the most prominent sites in the major arrondissements, with two days left over to fill in or to stroll, something one was advised to do in Paris, although Ellen is not by nature a stroller. On arrival, she discovered she could decipher street signs and menus and understand snippets of conversation, having assimilated some of her mother's tutorials.

After breakfast that morning, she took off to examine the neighborhood known as Le Marais, where she gaped at inscrutable street art and incongruous Hebrew lettering on shop signs in the aged Jewish district. She skipped the Picasso museum, because she can view his tangled images at the Fine Arts museum at home, if she chooses; however she sat for nearly an hour mesmerized by the fountain at Place des Vosges.

She stopped for lunch at a bistro with red leather banquettes and boorish waiters, and as she left, she tucked a leftover croissant and a wedge of cheese into a paper napkin and into her purse, for dinner.

At the next stop, Place de la Bastiille, she imagined the furtive lives that brought the less savory of people to incarceration there, like Sherlock Holmes' adversaries. She admired its formidability. From there, she hopped a bus to the Père Lachaise cemetery, where politicians, philosophers and artists shared the ground beneath her feet and where, she thought, her mother might have liked to be buried, as if, by sepulchral proximity, she might be elevated to loftier standing.

As Ellen returned to the hotel that evening, the rain, which had threatened every day, at last descended. She ran two blocks to the discreet hotel doorway and sprinted the four flights of stairs to her room, flopping on the hard bed to munch the croissant and cheese. As she changed into her nightgown, her eyes were drawn to a café below where two men and a woman, dressed in business suits, huddled at a table. Ellen wrapped a blanket over her shoulders – she chills easily and, paradoxically, overheats quickly – and then sat at the edge of the bed to watch them.

The only patrons seated outside, they ignored the weather, sheltered by an awning. They chatted exuberantly and laughed in unison. A waiter parsed their carafe of wine to each of their glasses before removing dishes and brushing the table free of crumbs. Coffee and pastry were served as they continued their intimate conversation, which she imagined went on long after she tired of the show and pulled the shade for the night.

So French, her mother would have said, to linger so long over a meal. Remarkable, Ellen thought, to have so much to say.

The following morning, the man at the breakfast table waved her over the moment she arrived. Not wanting to hurt his feelings, she sat.

Are you completely taken by the city? he asked.

Not taken, Ellen might have said, although she would have to admit she felt familiar now with the street map. She nodded with as much sincerity as possible.

Paris is a magnet. Once it has captured your polarity, you will be drawn back, again and again, he alleged.

To prove his point, he rotated his iPad toward her and scrolled through photographs. She watched a parade of plazas, bridges, turrets and archways, also chiseled faces, but to Ellen's eye, all tinged in gray.

You're a photographer? she asked.

A hobby. I'm a software developer. Twenty-five years. Not sure where the time goes. He sighed loudly. *I've taken a year off to chronicle a dance company migrating from one European capital to another. My sister was a dancer and...* He hesitated, as if something more personal might be disclosed, but said nothing else

237

about her. *This troupe, they're so young, from all over Europe, and no matter how much rehearsal, they never make the same move twice. I have thousands of images at practice and performance and each routine might as well be a snowflake. Not to mention their fantastically limber bodies, they sway like rubber, no, like reeds undulating in a marsh. No, no, that's not right either, because every move is choreographed, like a computer program, a sequence of ones and zeroes lined up just right.* He chuckled. *Actually, I'm reminded of middle school videos about reproduction. Remember those? Chromosomes crash into each other and split in a state of controlled chaos. A lot like modern dance.*

Ellen tried, but could not imagine dancers like chromosomes. *What will you do with the photographs?* she asked, certain there must be a purpose.

I've posted many to the company's website. And I've just put up a vlog called days of the dancers. Might get attention from the search engines.

Ellen had never met anyone so cavalier. She would no more have considered taking off a year and traipsing around with no intent than she would take flight into space.

Life is short, n'est ce pas? he said, with a smile so genuine Ellen couldn't help but smile in return and, without warning, he took her hand and she let him hold it, briefly, so as not to dampen his spirit.

His name was Byron French, which, he said, in that self-possessed way people say what they've said repeatedly, made him nearly a naturalized citizen of the country. He had recently turned fifty and had taken a two-week vacation every year since college to European capitals, always with a stop in Paris.

Now, he proclaimed proudly, *I recommend restaurants and day trips and I know just about every street in Paris worth knowing.*

For the next two days, after continental breakfast, Byron escorted Ellen to sites beyond her itinerary. They spent a morning wandering the Plantée, abandoned railway tracks transformed into an elevated park, where they gazed over rooftops and wobbled along a cable footbridge before descending to explore the artisan shops tucked into the arches below. At the Baccarat Museum, delicate sculpted glass glistened like ecclesiastical windows and at the Dupuytren, Ellen cringed at the anatomical oddities, like formaldehyde-preserved Siamese twins, her heart racing and stomach roiling, although she could not turn her eyes away.

Midday, they parked on benches at one or another of the city's lavish parks and chomped on baguette sandwiches wrapped in crinkly paper. When Ellen shivered in the wind, Byron removed the sapphire blue scarf wrapped Parisian-style around his thick neck to chivalrously cloak her shoulders and she felt instantly warmer.

Later in the day, while Byron photographed dancers in rehearsal, Ellen returned to her room, to the welcome silence, while the gray of the day shifted to a charcoal night.

Byron invited her to a dance performance at a theater tucked into a backstreet on the left bank. She dressed in the one skirt, with a body-hugging matching sweater she had tossed into her bag at the last minute, her mother's voice in her head urging her to *pretty-up now and then.*

From backstage, she watched the dancers' trim muscular bodies contort and rise to heights she'd never imagined. She couldn't conceive of how they do what they do and her head was spinning from the snappish moves and sultry music. After the performance, they joined the dancers for a late supper at a dimly lit restaurant where food was cheap and plentiful enough to feed their enormous post-performance appetites. Platters overflowed with aromatic cheeses, thinly sliced salted meats and herbed olives, and baskets were filled with crusty bread. The dancers gobbled the food as fast and loud as they babbled, so many speaking at once, in English and French, Dutch and German, Ellen barely made out a word.

Instead, she watched them. So young, such rosy skin and bright eyes, slender bodies and faces like porcelain dolls, although, between bites and banter, they chugged vodka or wine and smoked cigarettes, one after another. A girl named Faith, from Belgium, as sinewy and ethereal as a line drawing, with sparkling inquisitive eyes, assailed Ellen in crystal-clear clipped English with a barrage of personal questions.

No, I have never been out of the country before, Ellen answered. *No, I've never seen modern dance, only Swan Lake and The Nutcracker. No, I'm not familiar with Miles Davis or Nina Simone,* the soundtrack for the dancers that night. *No, I never took dance lessons or music lessons or painting,* she muttered, tiring of the negative, the disclosure of a limited life.

Alors, what is your passion? Faith cried with discernible frustration, determined to mine the jewel she believed must be hiding beneath Ellen's lackluster casing.

If Ellen were to answer that maintaining a perfectly organized file system for tax forms and client returns was her specialty, Faith would have laughed. Or that she took pride in methodically grouping emails in archived folders, because Ellen's boss, an accounting wizard, was, in this, muddled. Could a dancer possibly comprehend Ellen's greatest achievement? Winning the eighth grade spelling bee with the word vivisepulture, a word foreign go her then, but which she broke down into syllables and reconstructed correctly. Or that she dispensed with her mother's will so promptly and efficiently, the county clerk commended her skill, after which she packed her few precious possessions – her father's Timex watch, a silver cross on a delicate chain, a worn copy of *Les Miserables* – into a fireproof box she buried in a crevice beneath the stairway for a seeker from the future to find.

Accomplishments, of a sort, yes. Passion? No. Not an emotion with which Ellen was familiar. Even under cover of darkness, when she silently satisfied the urgings of her body, there was no passion, merely competence.

Could she ever explain to such an artistic creature the exquisite pleasure of precision? On the other hand, watching from the wings that night, dance seemed all about precision. Every move synchronized. And when the dancers landed out of sight of the audience, panting and sweating, cursing a mistake only they knew they'd made, they would suddenly lift their wings to fly back to center stage, back into the graceful exactness of the choreography.

Perhaps she and the dancers, and Byron, had something in common after all.

Late that night, Ellen woke to the window frame rattling against a brisk wind. She had been dreaming of streams cascading down waterfalls and into crystal-blue pools, and she recalled a list she had made long ago, one of those things young girls do, of all the places she might someday see. She had itemized locations alphabetically: Bora Bora, Costa Rica, the Galapagos and Morocco, on to Sedona, Tanzania, and Wellington, sites she discovered in library copies of *National Geographic*. No museums, no boulevards or gray skies, rather immense boulders, towering trees and free-falling water, and in that moment in the darkness, Ellen concluded she had absolutely nothing in common with her mother.

She might have come to that realization earlier in life, but Ellen has never had the inclination to introspection. She was a satisfactory student and a dependable daughter and after she earned a certificate in administration, she accepted a post at a small firm a twenty-minute train ride from home, where she works to this day, eighteen years later, and where, to be kind, they call her the Office Manager.

She sleeps still in the dormered bedroom her father carved for her in the attic, in a part of town where the houses are packed together like boxes in shipping crates, cries of dreamers and angry spouses reverberating like sound waves. She has spent a lifetime gazing out her window at identical postage-stamp lawns which, over time, filled with taller trees and mature flowering bushes, and the houses with young families.

The day after tax day, with her boss's blessing, she flew to Paris to fulfill her mother's dying wish and now, here she was, in a dingy hotel room, listening to raindrops punctuate the discordant snores of the stranger squeezed next to her in the narrow bed.

Byron had escorted her to her door that night and took her face in his hands, staring into her eyes before he kissed her, tenderly, despite the scratch of the beard, and after the kiss, his face so close she saw the tiny red lines within the longing in his eyes, he asked, *may I?* Ellen nodded and led him into her room.

In a matter of moments, he had removed her clothes and eased her onto the bed, draping the blanket over her while he disrobed. When he joined her, he nestled close to keep her warm, their bodies pressed together until she stopped shivering from the cold, trembling instead from his intrepid fingers in places so rarely touched by other hands. When first she, then he, climaxed, Ellen bit her lip so hard to stay quiet she drew blood, which Byron licked away with delight.

He was not Ellen's first lover. She has been sleeping for three years with an accountant hired on during the busy tax season. He resides for two months each spring at a short-term rental where she spends the weekends with him. He disclosed from the first he is unhappily married, but he would never abandon his children. Ellen respected his honesty and steadfastness. She told her mother she had to work late into the night most of the season and was put up at a company apartment near the office and Ellen suspected she knew there was more to the story; however, by not prying, or censuring, conveyed tacit approval, gratified, perhaps, that her daughter showed a touch of pluck. After all, an affair is so Parisian, yet something her mother would no more do than go to Paris on her own.

The accountant was a capable lover, while Byron was fervent and eclectic, which Ellen found as fascinating as the oddities at the museum, although she wondered that night if she too was some sort of freak – capable of experiencing a romantic rendezvous in Paris with little more than a modicum of gratification.

The next morning, her last morning in Paris, Byron proposed she travel with him on the rest of the dancers' tour. The company manager had offered him a position as official photographer, his compensation in accommodations.

They have two days respite for rehearsals and three performances in Brussels before they go to Amsterdam, then on to Vienna and Prague, and ultimately Dubrovnik. Oh Ellen, you cannot imagine the beauty of the Croatian coast!

Ellen was shocked at the suggestion. *But I have to go back to work.*

Why?

Because that's what I do. I have responsibility, I have a house.

The house will wait, he said, as if an obvious solution to a mathematical equation.

How will I live? Ellen cried.

Bunk with me and we'll share expenses. You must have a few dollars saved, you won't need much. This is our time for an adventure!

Take off without purpose? Madness, Ellen thought, as she considered how to word her rebuttal, but before she could speak, Byron posed an alternative.

Just start in Brussels. We'll drink coffee with chocolate sprinkled on top and consume huge bowls of mussels with every possible variety of beer. If you're not delighted, go home, or we'll go on from there.

Because his facial expression was so hopeful, his voice pleading, Byron seemed a small boy hungering for a bicycle. Who was she to deny him? No more than she could deny her mother's wish to see Paris.

'*You have only one real duty in life... to save your dream,*' Byron recited. *Modigliani said that, my mantra since my sister died last year,* he explained, beseeching Ellen with an intimate confession. *You would have liked each other.*

Although Ellen was struck by his need to recreate something of his sister's life, she was certain she could not share that dream. She has never had, nor expects to have, nor does she believe she needs to have a fantasy of her own, only the satisfaction, the privilege, now and then, of making others' lives more pleasing.

In truth, if she wanted to disappear for a time, she would hike through a rain forest or swim under a mountain waterfall, all of which she knew she lacked the courage to do.

What have you got to lose? Byron implored.

His plea reminded Ellen of a winter day, long ago, when her mother shouted the same words as Ellen skidded on the edges of a frozen pond, hoping her nine year-old daughter might master a winter sport. When Ellen's scrawny legs locked at the knees and ankles flattened to the ice, she clutched the makeshift fence along the perimeter, afraid to go too near the center, where skaters seemed to dance effortlessly. Her mother sat on the bleachers with other mothers, wrapped in plaid wool blankets and gripping thermoses filled with hot chocolate, yelling in despair to her timid child.

Stand up, Ellen. What have you got to lose?

After Ellen had fallen once too often, her butt bruised and toes nearly frozen, her mother wordlessly ushered her home and in that moment, confirmed in many subsequent moments, Ellen accepted as general principle that she was better suited to sticking close to the edges, rather than stumble into the thick of things.

To her surprise, and his, Ellen surrendered to Byron's plea. She dispatched an email to her boss requesting permission to prolong her sabbatical with the reassurance she would be back in time for the fall audit season. She told Byron she had every intention of keeping that promise.

That night, she rinsed her clothes in the tiny sink at the hotel and spread them out on the heating pipes to dry while they took off for their last outing.

They strolled the Tuilleries Garden, where stately trees revealed new blooms, after which they took in a candlelight concert at the church at St. Germaine des Prés. As a choir bellowed gospel music to the spires, blasting their passion to the heavens, Ellen sat very still, absorbing their melodious voices, while Byron swayed to the tempo as if the rhythm of his heart.

The following morning, after their last continental breakfast, they took the Metro to the Gare du Nord to board a train to Brussels. They arrived early and parked on a bench near the giant departure board anchoring the station. Ellen sat with their suitcases while Byron snapped photographs of a young girl, eight or nine, wearing a camel coat and a matching bonnet capped over long wavy tresses, a flower pinned to the rim. Byron turned now and then to share a smile.

So easily pleased, this man, Ellen thought, still amazed she was on her way to places she never planned to see. Perhaps her mother would like her better now.

Her eyes drifted to the overhead departure board listing destinations and gates. No computer monitor in that historic terminal, rather wooden squares imprinted with letters and numerals, shifting position by the second, the top line evaporating as each train departed, the next to board clattering into its place and, every time, schedules fluttered briefly in limbo until the detail spelled out: hour, minutes, terminus and gate, routes constantly flapping before snapping into position.

Ellen watched. Mesmerized. As spellbound as she was backstage the night of the dance performance. She ignored the swarm of travelers rushing to catch trains or meet arrivals, on their paths to or from, as she was now, all oblivious to the choreography of alphanumerics spiraling into meaning, as harmonious and precise as a dance.

She felt, in that moment, curiously serene - entranced by the environs, by the contrast between precision and chaos, like Byron, like the dancers, like an unforeseen future, like the symmetry of this elegant city, and she closed her eyes to obliterate all noise and movement other than the syncopation of the travel board, its ebb and flow remarkably evocative of water flowing over a rocky precipice to a pristine pool below.

END

Acknowledgments

To those for whom reason forever wrestles with the heart:
These stories are for you.

For Dana and Julie and the boys:
Spenser, Aslan & Christopher, Sean & Mauricio

For Paul: Reason & Passion

Thanks to the readers
Chris, Deana, Deborah, Joe, Kevin, Linda, Paul & Susan.
[Especially Deborah and Chris for multiple readings.]

Thanks to the cheerleaders
Carol, Robyn, Marianna, Laura, CQ, Leslie/Andrew, Byron,
Ginger/Joe, Roberta, Amy, Vince, Andrea, Joanne, Carole,
Liz, Ilene, Hollie, Babs, Joy, Edie, Val, Nadine & Cynthia.

Respects to
Caravaggio, Arthur Conan Doyle, W. E. B. Du Bois,
William Faulkner, John Irving, Keats, Margaret Mead,
Michelangelo, Modigliani, Toni Morrison, NPR,
Picasso, Ayn Rand, Shonda Rhimes, Christina Rossetti,
Alice Walker & D. W. Winnicott

Hugs to Diva Diane of Diane's Books of Greenwich
& friends at Laguna Beach Books.

About the Author

Randy Kraft is a former newspaper and magazine journalist and also a business strategist/writer. She writes book reviews [OC BookBlog} for OC Insite, a culture and entertainment website in southern California, where she resides. She earned a Bachelor's degree in English from Hunter College, NY and a Master's in Writing from Manhattanville College, NY.

Two novels have been published:
"Colors of the Wheel" [2014]
"Signs of Life" [2016].
A play, "Off Season" was produced at the San Miguel de Allende, MX, first short play festival [2013].

"Rational Women" is her first collection of short stories and four have appeared in literary magazines.

randykraftwriter.com